Aberdeenshire Libraries
www.aberdeenshire.gov.uk/libraries
Renewals Hotline 01224 661511
Downloads available from
www.aberdeenshirelibraries.lib.overdrive.com

⌐DQUARTERS

2 0 SEP 2016

HEADQUARTERS

2 0 OCT 2016
1 4 FEB 2017

0 4 JUL 2017

0 6 FEB 2018

2 1 SEP 2018

1 2 AUG 2023

D0228768

Dear Reader,

Thank you for picking up a copy of *Tempting Nashville's Celebrity Doc*.

I grew up watching *Hee Haw* on Saturday night at my grandparents' house. The first musicians I was exposed to as a child were Cash, Carter, Jones and Hank Williams Jr. Country was a part of my childhood.

Even though I never really thought much about Nashville when I grew up, I couldn't pass up the opportunity to visit on my way to RT Booklovers Convention New Orleans in 2014.

The moment I crossed the Tennessee border I fell absolutely in love with the state and the city. I knew that I had to set a book there, and I wanted to incorporate the music I love so much into the story—which is how my neurosurgeon Dr Reece Castle came to be.

He walked into my mind a couple of years ago, when I was in Nashville, and like the true gentleman he was he waited until I could tell his and Vivian's story.

I hope you enjoy their story—and if you ever get the chance to spend a bit of time in Nashville, or even the great state of Tennessee, I hope you do it. You won't regret it.

I love hearing from readers, so please drop by my website amyruttan.com or give me a shout on Twitter @ruttanamy.

With warmest wishes,

Amy Ruttan

TEMPTING NASHVILLE'S CELEBRITY DOC

BY
AMY RUTTAN

All rights reserved including the right of reproduction in whole
or in part in any form. This edition is published by arrangement with
Harlequin Books S.A.

This is a work of fiction. Names, characters, places, locations and
incidents are purely fictional and bear no relationship to any real
life individuals, living or dead, or to any actual places, business
establishments, locations, events or incidents. Any resemblance is
entirely coincidental.

This book is sold subject to the condition that it shall not, by way of
trade or otherwise, be lent, resold, hired out or otherwise circulated
without the prior consent of the publisher in any form of binding or
cover other than that in which it is published and without a similar
condition including this condition being imposed on the subsequent
purchaser.

® and TM are trademarks owned and used by the trademark owner
and/or its licensee. Trademarks marked with ® are registered with the
United Kingdom Patent Office and/or the Office for Harmonisation in
the Internal Market and in other countries.

Published in Great Britain 2016
By Mills & Boon, an imprint of HarperCollins*Publishers*
1 London Bridge Street, London, SE1 9GF

© 2016 Amy Ruttan

ISBN: 978-0-263-06515-2

Our policy is to use papers that are natural, renewable and recyclable
products and made from wood grown in sustainable forests. The logging
and manufacturing processes conform to the legal environmental
regulations of the country of origin.

Printed and bound in Great Britain
by CPI Antony Rowe, Chippenham, Wiltshire

ROM

Born and raised just outside Toronto, Canada, **Amy Ruttan** fled the big city to settle down with the country boy of her dreams. After the birth of her second child Amy was lucky enough to realise her lifelong dream of becoming a romance author. When she's not furiously typing away at her computer she's mum to three wonderful children who use her as a personal taxi and chef.

Books by Amy Ruttan

Mills & Boon Medical Romance

Visit the Author Profile page at millsandboon.co.uk for more titles.

This book is dedicated to all the country greats,
new and old, who have touched my heart.
Thank you for the music.

Also to my father, who introduced me
to the music of Cash and Hank Williams Jr.
I may not have appreciated it when I was younger,
but I get it now. Thanks, Dad.

Praise for
Amy Ruttan

'Amy Ruttan delivers an entertaining read that
transports readers into a world of blissful romance set
amidst the backdrop of the medical field. Sharp, witty
and descriptive, *One Night in New York* is sure to keep
readers turning the pages!'

—*Contemporary Romance Reviews*

'I highly recommend this read for all fans of romance
reads with amazing, absolutely breathtaking scenes,
to die for dialogue, and everything else that is needed
to make this a beyond awesome and *wow* read!'

—*Goodreads* on
Melting the Ice Queen's Heart

CHAPTER ONE

"YOU CAN DO THIS." It was a reassurance she kept repeating over and over to herself. And though she didn't usually talk to herself in public, saying it out loud made her feel better.

Yeah, right.

Right now, standing here, all her bravado was fleeting as she stared up at the impressive entrance of the Cumberland Mills Memorial Hospital. The hospital where she'd done her first residency, before she'd left for her prestigious fellowship in Munich seven years ago.

Nothing had changed. She closed her eyes and took in the sweet, heady floral scent of the magnolia trees. It made her think of summers running barefoot on the lawn, of her father sitting in the swing on the wraparound porch strumming on his guitar while she played. A jangled memory of a man who'd left her and her mother a long time ago tied to the scent in the air.

She sighed and shook that thought out of her head. There was no room for those thoughts today. No room for memories.

Though that was difficult. Everywhere she went in Nashville she was reminded of the ghosts of her past. The choices she'd made and the hurt she'd left behind. Nashville haunted her, which was why she'd left. Why she'd planned to never come back.

Except here she was. Back at the beginning.

You're here for Mama. You're not starting over.

Still, coming back to the place she grew up felt like a second chance. As if karma was telling her she'd made all the wrong choices and was making her start all over again.

She had to remind herself that things were different. *She* was different. She was stronger. When she'd started here she was so unsure of herself that she had put on an air of confidence, built walls to keep people out. So much so she was considered an ice queen by some, while the seasoned surgeons thought she was too meek to be good at what she did.

Only one person had seen through all that.

Don't think about him.

Vivian steeled her resolve and clutched the strap of her designer messenger bag. She was no longer that girl from the east side of Nashville, the girl from the wrong side of the tracks. She was now a world-class neurosurgeon and diagnostician.

She held her head up high and walked through the doors of Cumberland Mills, taking in the sights of one of the busiest and most affluent hospitals in Nashville.

Nothing had changed on the inside.

Like me.

"Dr. Maguire, it's good to see you again."

Vivian turned to see the Chief of Surgery, Dr. Isaac Brigham, walking toward her across the spacious atrium, the heart of the hospital. Other than a bit more gray in his ebony hair, Dr. Brigham still looked like how she remembered. When he'd been an Attending and she'd been a scared resident trying to melt into the background. How quickly she'd changed under his tutelage.

"Never forget you're a shark. Always moving forward."

That was what Dr. Brigham taught her and she'd taken it

to her heart when she'd decided to look forward and go to Germany.

Only today she didn't feel so much like a shark, standing here at the beginning again.

Vivian took his hand and shook it. "So good to see you again, Dr. Brigham." Only that was a lie. Dr. Brigham might have taught her to be a shark, might have been a good surgeon, but he was two-faced and stubborn. You didn't want to get on his bad side.

It was trying for her to play nice with a man she found so annoying. A man she didn't trust.

"It's Isaac." He had that plummy Belle Meade accent, affluent. So different from the accent she'd worked hard to get rid of. The one people looked down their noses at. Judging her as if she was trash and someone who didn't belong.

She smiled. "I think that will be hard for me. I mean, you did set me on my path to that fellowship in Munich. You were my teacher and I was terrified of you."

Isaac chuckled and crossed his arms. "Scare you? I've heard stories from your time in Munich. Have to say, I knew that you had it in you. Though I had moments of doubt. You were so quiet and shy. You barely spoke above a whisper back then."

"I don't whisper anymore." Vivian smiled to herself, pleased that her reputation was preceding her, because she knew she had to build up a reputation here. She was after Dr. Brigham's job. It was no secret that he was planning on retiring and most of the senior surgeons here had an advantage over her. They were known, they had a history. Most came from old Nashville money and she wasn't a fool. She knew that would be an advantage to them and she was an unknown entity. Something she planned to change.

"Well, I'll take you around our Neuro department and introduce you to your VIP patient."

Vivian fell into step beside him. "VIP patient?"

He nodded. "Well, you have to get your feet wet here. Besides, I hear you're the best diagnostician."

"So they tell me," she said. "Tell me about the case."

"You'll be working on the case with one of my most respected neurosurgeons. It's a strange case and what better way to initiate your time here as our top diagnostician."

"Most respected neurosurgeon" meant one thing to Vivian. Competition.

"Who is the VIP patient?"

"Country star Gary Trainer. He's a rising star, but has been having the most curious neurological symptoms since he was rushed in two days ago."

"Has he had an MRI?"

Isaac grinned. "Of course—as I said, he's a VIP patient and his record label is very anxious to get him back on his tour."

Of course.

Musicians were always eager to get back on the road. She'd heard her dad say that enough times.

"Stay longer, Hank. Please. Just a bit longer."

"I can't, Sandra. I need to be on the road. I have to make it. I will make it, just like Ray Castille. I will be as big as he is."

Vivian laughed uneasily, trying to shake her father's voice from her head. "Musicians."

Isaac nodded and they got on an elevator, riding in silence until they got up to the top floor. The doors opened with a ding and they stepped off. "This is where our VIP patients stay while they're inpatients here."

Vivian didn't respond. It made her stomach knot just a bit. Money talked here. There were times when she was a kid when they couldn't get the help they needed. And she recalled the hours she and Mama had waited in an overcrowded, dingy ER.

Then there were the medical bills after her mother's

suicide attempt that took years to pay off because the ambulance took her to a hospital they couldn't afford.

Vivian tried to give back when she could. Still, seeing the luxury of Cumberland Mills VIP wing made her wonder how much old money was invested into this instead of the pro bono fund.

She followed Isaac down the hall toward the end room. She could see a group of eager surgical interns in the room from the open door, obviously on rounds, and she couldn't help but wonder who her competition was. And frankly she didn't care. She'd easily push whoever it was out of the running when she diagnosed Mr. Trainer and got him back out on tour in front of his fans.

Dr. Brigham knocked on the door. "Mind if we interrupt?"

"Not at all, Doc. They tell me you brought in a specialist all the way from Germany to deal with my case," a sweet, deep Georgian voice answered.

Isaac nodded. "Only the best for you, Mr. Trainer."

Vivian stepped around the door, her smile quickly fading as she met the gaze of the attending doctor who was standing next to Mr. Trainer's bed.

Those familiar brown eyes, pinning her to the spot. He had a bit of scruff and his hair wasn't as long. The short hair suited him. And he wasn't as gangly and lean as he'd been when they'd been residents. That young boyish face had melted away. He was more hardened, mature, but it was still him and he was still as handsome as ever.

Reece.

She'd met him in her final year of residency. He'd transferred in from a different hospital, brought in by Dr. Brigham. He was the only one who'd seen through her walls. He'd been her compass back then. Her foundation.

"Who cares where you came from? It's where you're going that matters."

Don't think about him. Only she couldn't help but think about him as he was standing in the same room with her. Even though she'd made the decision to leave, she thought of him every day. She'd wronged him and he knew that. Vivian put her career first and she always would.

She could rely on her talent, medicine and herself. She put no faith in love or hearts, because hearts were so easily broken. Something she'd witnessed firsthand when her dad left.

Relationships were never on her radar but, from the first moment she'd met Reece, she'd forgotten that.

The memory came into her mind now...

"Tired?"

"Yes. It was a long shift. I needed air." She had closed her eyes and hoped that he would leave, but he'd lingered. "Can I help you, Dr. Castle?"

He had shrugged. "I needed air too. I love the scent of magnolias."

"Yeah, me too. It reminds me of home."

"Where are you from?" he'd asked.

"Nashville." She hadn't known why she was engaging in a conversation with him.

"Me too."

Then he'd reached up in the tree and plucked a large blossom. Before she'd been able to protest he'd put it behind her ear. A shiver of anticipation had raced down her spine. His strong hand had rested on her cheek.

"What're you doing?" The words had been a whisper because she'd lost her voice, embarrassed that he was paying attention to her.

"I don't know. It just suits you."

Even now, after seven years, she could still feel the memory of his hand against her cheek, holding her still as he pinned that bloom in her hair. She also remembered how much she had wanted to kiss him in that moment.

How his touch had affected her.

She couldn't believe he was still here in Nashville. She'd thought he would've taken some exciting offer from a bigger city. Even though he'd always said he wanted to stay in Nashville, she'd never quite believed him. He was a talented surgeon. He must've had other offers over the years. So she was shocked to see him here. The only person she'd ever opened up to. The man who threatened to steal her heart.

Did he remember? That's why you left.

Vivian had panicked when she fell so deeply in love with him. She had no control over herself when it came to him. Which was why when the Munich job came up she took it.

Love was not something she ever wanted and after leaving Reece it was not something she deserved. And she couldn't stay in Nashville, but Reece had made it clear he wanted roots. Permanent roots. And that scared her. She didn't want roots or permanency, because that didn't last. She didn't believe in it.

And she only had to look to her parents to see that.

So she'd slipped away to Germany. She'd left him a note but, by the way those dark brown eyes bored into her with cool disdain, it was apparent to her a note had *not* been enough.

Distance had done no good. She thought of him all the time, regretted what had happened. She'd never expected to find him still here, still working for Dr. Brigham. He had so much potential. Why couldn't he see it? He was too damn talented to stay here.

Roots be damned; why was he still here wasting his talent? Not that Cumberland Mills wasn't a great hospital, but it wasn't the leading hospital for neurosurgery. If Reece had moved somewhere to specialize he could have done so much more for their field.

"Dr. Castle and Mr. Trainer, I would like to introduce you both to Dr. Vivian Maguire. She's a specialist in neurosurgery and an excellent diagnostician, having studied under Dr. Mannheim at the Munich Center for Neuroscience." Dr. Brigham puffed out his chest. "She was one of my residents as well."

"I remember," Reece said finally, his voice cold, causing a shudder to run down her spine. "We were in the same class."

Warmth flooded her cheeks and she nodded. "Yes, Dr. Castle and I were in the same class our last year of residency, Dr. Brigham."

Dr. Brigham's brows furrowed and then he nodded. "That's right. I'd completely forgotten. My apologies. So you two already know each other. That's wonderful."

Wonderful.

Yeah, they knew each other, but the way that Reece was looking at her was like she was a stranger. Cold. Detached.

Can you blame him?

She deserved it.

That was not the Reece Castle she remembered but, then again, seven years was a long time ago and she'd changed too.

"Well, I don't think I've had the pleasure of meeting my new doctor," Gary Trainer said, flashing her a smile which was charming and probably just a bit dangerous to all those rabid fans.

Vivian took his outstretched hand and gave it a squeeze, doing her own little test. Gary squeezed back, or he tried, but there wasn't any strength to his grip, the muscles were rigid and there was a tremble. Slight, but it was there.

Maybe someone not trained wouldn't notice it, but Vivian did.

"It's a pleasure to meet you, Mr. Trainer. I look forward to working with your present medical team." She glanced up quickly at Reece, but he wasn't looking at her. He was scrolling through the chart on the computer tablet.

Avoidance. She knew it well. He didn't like to be the center of attention; he didn't like awkward situations. He avoided them at all costs. He might have told her to be strong and speak out, but he didn't do the same for himself. He didn't like the spotlight or change.

His appearance had changed, but Reece was still the same.

Reece knew that she was looking at him and he didn't care one bit.

Liar.

He couldn't believe it was her. He'd known that a diagnostician with a neurosurgery background was being flown in from Germany, but it had never occurred to him that it would be Vivian. And now, looking at her, Reece wasn't even sure he recognized her. In seven years she'd gone from a shy, cold, detached woman to one with confidence exuding from her pores.

Or arrogance.

Her unruly red hair was swept back and tamed in a bun. She was polished, wearing designer clothes, but, as he stared into her green eyes, the costume couldn't hide from him that girl who'd grown up on the wrong side of the tracks was there still.

The woman who preferred blue jeans and running barefoot through the grass.

The woman he'd fallen in love with. This facade just reminded him that version of Vivian he loved was gone and this Vivian was a stranger. It pained him to be around her.

When they'd been residents together, she'd constantly talked about working with Dr. Mannheim. It had been her dream, not his, but he'd foolishly thought that love would keep her here, that she wouldn't go. She'd planned to leave Nashville far behind her. Still, Reece wasn't the only one who built up walls. He was closed off, but Vivian ran from her problems.

The morning he'd rolled over and found her note had crushed him. Vivian had left, and hadn't asked him to go with her. What made it worse was the engagement ring he'd bought for her—the one he had to return the next day—because the morning she'd left was when he was going to open up to her. Tell her everything. Things he didn't tell anyone.

If she had asked him to go, he would've gone with her. *Only you wouldn't have.*

Germany was not what he wanted.

At least that was what he'd told himself to justify her leaving. To make himself believe that was the only reason why she hadn't asked him and why he wouldn't have gone.

Only he'd been lying to himself. He might've gone, but he was never given the choice. The fact was that she hadn't wanted him to go with her. Plain and simple.

It still stung, even after all this time.

She'd been his best friend. The one person he'd opened up to. The only person who'd been able to get through his walls—and look what happened. She'd left.

He'd learned his lesson well.

He wasn't going to make that same mistake twice. People didn't get second chances, if what happened between him and his father was anything to go by.

"Well, shoot, you're just a sight for sore eyes," Gary said, smiling again. "No offense, Dr. Castle, but I do get tired of looking at your ugly mug every day."

Reece chuckled, his residents snickering behind him. When he glanced up at Vivian there was a pink tinge to her cheeks. Vivian was never the one for compliments. She used to think compliments could be confused as a form of weakness or she still didn't think she deserved them. Only the compliments were valid. She was beautiful. He'd forgotten how much so. His memories didn't do justice to her.

He'd forgotten about how coppery her hair was in certain lights, how green her eyes were. Like emeralds. The subtle smattering of freckles across her nose against her creamy white skin.

She was tall. Elegant.

Sexy as hell still.

She broke your heart.

He had to keep reminding himself of that. Under all that soft beauty she was just as hardened as he was.

When he'd met her she was shy and timid, but always closed off, but then he'd fallen in love with her. Completely—to the point he didn't have to hide who he was. He'd adored her and he'd foolishly thought she felt the same. Good thing he didn't tell her who he really was... Love wasn't strong enough to keep her. He should've known better, given who his mother was. Women couldn't be trusted.

He knew Vivian came from a very different world to the one which he had grown up in. She was just as secretive about her past as he was and they hadn't talked much about their childhood, other than he knew they'd both raised themselves and didn't have much of one. Then again, who needed talk when they had sex?

Now, seven years later, he couldn't remember why they'd been friends or what they had in common, but they'd been drawn to each other. They'd clung to each other, both starved of love perhaps? He'd let his guard down around her.

"I appreciate the sentiment, Gary." Then he briefly shared a quick glance with Vivian. "You're right about Dr. Maguire being easier on the eyes."

Vivian's blush deepened and the smile disappeared. She was clearly uncomfortable and he was treading on dangerous ground. That was the last thing he needed, to bandy words with Vivian here in front of his patient and residents. He had to work with her and he was professional. Besides, there was nothing left to say. It was all in the past.

Is it?

"Well, I better make myself better acquainted with the neurosurgical staff and find my office. It was a pleasure to meet you, Mr. Trainer."

"Gary please, Dr. Maguire."

"Gary, then." She shook his hand and glanced up at Reece. "Dr. Castle, I'll speak with you later, I'm sure."

Reece didn't answer; he just nodded quickly. He watched her walk out the door, feeling slightly guilty about how cold he'd been to her.

She's the competition.

He had to remind himself that, even if he wasn't particularly interested in going after Dr. Brigham's job, he hadn't worked all these years pouring his blood, sweat, soul and tears into the neuro program at Cumberland Mills to have someone like Vivian waltz in and take it over. She had to prove herself to him. He had Dr. Brigham's ear. And if she wanted to run the surgical program she had to prove to him and everyone else she was here for the long haul.

Vivian had left for greener pastures years ago. Back then she didn't see Cumberland Mills as much. Just a stepping stone. Reece really knew what this hospital was about. He didn't know why she was back other than to take Dr. Brigham's job.

Your job.

He shook that thought away. He'd been offered the job but he didn't want it. He didn't need it and didn't want to live up to Dr. Brigham's reputation. Some shadows were too big to step out of and Reece's dad had made it clear time and time again he didn't have what it took. It wasn't his job, nor was it hers.

Vivian's return to Nashville was just a blip. An annoyance. She was not a threat, she was not competition and definitely she was no longer a temptation.

Keep telling yourself that.

CHAPTER TWO

"WELL, I NEVER thought I'd see your face here again."

Startled, Vivian glanced up to see Reece standing in the door of her office, his arms crossed and leaning casually against the doorjamb. Those dark eyes were trained on her, but the sparkle he once shared with her was gone. Still, he was just as handsome as ever. Something about him made her heart beat just a bit faster. She'd thought that being apart from him would dissipate the attraction she'd always had for him. She was wrong.

So wrong.

Which was probably why any relationship she'd had since had been fleeting and not worth a second glance because now, staring at Reece, she knew no man could ever affect her the way Reece had.

She hadn't heard him come into her office but, then again, he always had a way of sneaking up on her, or nurses, or doctors. As if he moved at the edge of the shadows, unnoticed until he wanted to be seen.

When she'd asked him about it once he'd said offhandedly he'd learned to do that as a child, but never really elaborated further on that. Of course, Reece never did elaborate much on his past. She only knew he was from Nashville. That was it. And she never went on about her past. All he knew was she grew up on the wrong side of the tracks and he didn't. Though he'd never specified and that was the way they wanted it.

"Past is past, Vivian. Let's focus on the now."

"Neither did I," she answered, folding her hands on the desk in front of her as if that would help protect her from him. "I am surprised to see *you're* still here…"

"Well, I wasn't offered a chance to study under Dr. Mannheim." There was a hint of bitterness to his voice, but really she wasn't surprised. Over the years working as Dr. Mannheim's protégée she'd dealt with a lot of people who were envious of her position.

People who also voiced their opinions that she didn't deserve it.

That she didn't earn it.

That she'd slept her way in, but none of that was true. They would know it wasn't true if they met Dr. Mannheim's life partner.

Still, there was always an undercurrent of jealousy. Working with Dr. Mannheim had been a huge honor and she wasn't sorry for taking it. She'd needed to get away from Nashville. She had to protect her heart.

"You could've had a similar opportunity, but you never pursued anything. In fact I'm surprised to see you still here. I thought you would've moved away. Find a greener pasture for your surgical skill to flourish."

Reece's eyes narrowed. "I was needed here. I never wanted to leave Nashville. As I recall, you were the one who was ready to leave this place at a moment's notice. Greener pastures never impressed me much."

"I didn't come back here to argue with you," Vivian said. "I don't regret leaving. I came here to work."

His expression was like thunder and she instantly regretted her words. Reece shut the door and then took a seat in the one and only chair that didn't have a ton of papers or a box on it.

"Of course. You're right, Vivian. Whether we like it or not, we're working together on this. Past is past. Let's focus on the now and our patient."

She nodded, relieved but also disappointed…

What was that about?

She was here to work, not dredge up the past. Coming back home to Nashville was bad enough; she didn't need old feelings getting in the way.

"So why don't we get to work, then?" she asked.

"Sure," he said, leaning back in the chair. "What would you like to talk about?"

"Why don't you fill me in on Mr. Trainer's case?"

"Signs and symptoms point to Parkinson's, but…"

"His test came back negative, I take it?"

Reece nodded. "Yes, even though really it's too soon to tell and hard to diagnose Parkinson's in the early stages."

"Do you know when the symptoms first started? Has he given you a history?"

Reece nodded. "He did and the symptoms only started out of the blue the other day when he collapsed on stage. That was two days ago."

"Sudden onset?" she asked, confused, as the thousands of possibilities swirled in her brain.

"Yes. He collapsed during a performance with what looked like an epileptic seizure. As you can tell from his MRI." Reece handed her a computer pad, an MRI on the screen. "It's clear of epileptic seizure activity."

Vivian stared at the MRI, instantly assessing the images in front of her, like she'd done a thousand times before. Like she'd done about three months ago when her mother's MRI showed up in her inbox and she could see the clear markers for early onset Alzheimer's.

"Don't you worry about me, baby girl. You stay in Germany. Finish your trial. Your work is important."

It was the tone which had scared her. The shake in her

mother's voice behind the facade of happiness. The same tone she'd used that terrible night Vivian had found her mother bleeding on the kitchen floor. So even though her mother had said she was okay, Vivian knew she wasn't.

Vivian owed it to her mother to come back home. Her mom had been her only constant in her life. She had sacrificed so much so Vivian could create a future for herself—so she didn't have to rely on someone else. That was what her mom had always said. In other words, a life where she didn't have to rely on a man.

"You don't need a man, Vivian. You're smart, talented. Don't let anyone hold you back."

Her mom's words had made her decide to go to Germany in the first place. She had wavered over it and for one brief moment she'd thought about putting down roots with Reece. Her mother had changed her mind.

She was very well aware that her mother's singing career had been held back by her father. A father who couldn't even be bothered to stick around. Her mother gave up a huge contract because Vivian's father had been jealous of his wife's success and then when he was offered a gig he was gone.

And that was the last they saw of him and their savings.

She couldn't leave her mother high and dry. She couldn't let her mother, who had early onset Alzheimer's, live out the rest of her life in a rundown facility while she was halfway across the world.

Vivian might be cutthroat when it came to her career, but she loved her mother. Loved her enough to come back to Nashville.

"Vivian, you okay?"

She shook her head, chasing those thoughts away. "Sorry?"

"You zoned out. I thought perhaps you saw something

I might've missed," Reece said, a hint of concern in his voice. She didn't deserve him. Never had.

"No, sorry. Jet lag." She passed the tablet back to Reece. "I think I would like another MRI done and an EEG monitor for a forty-eight hour period. Perhaps we can force a seizure in a controlled and monitored environment."

Reece nodded. "Sounds good, but how do you propose we do that when we don't know what triggered it?"

"You said he had a seizure on stage at the concert, right?"

"Yes, he did."

"How about we start with flashing lights, dark room and loud music?"

A small grin crept across Reece's face. It was good to see him smile. "Good thinking. I'll get my team of residents on it."

"Thanks. I'm glad you have the team of residents so readily at your disposal." It was so easy to talk to him about medicine. She'd forgotten. It was how they'd first connected. How he'd gotten through her defenses.

"Well, all the surgeons do. It's just I've been using them more often for my Alzheimer's trial study."

Vivian perked up. "Alzheimer's study?"

Reece nodded. "Yes, I have a trial running now with some medication therapy and electrotherapy with EEG monitoring for brain activity. I just started it."

"Have you found all your participants?" Vivian asked.

Reece frowned and cocked an eyebrow. "Why are you so interested?"

"Don't get on the defensive. Alzheimer's is not my specialty. I was merely making conversation."

Reece stared at her in disbelief, but then relaxed. "Yes, my trial is currently full. There is a large pool of people suffering from early onset Alzheimer's who are more than willing to participate."

Vivian tried not to show her disappointment, but really it was to be expected. Alzheimer's trials filled up quickly.

"So not interested in Alzheimer's, but here to take Dr. Brigham's job?" he asked.

The question caught her off guard. "Who told you that?"

"I'm not obtuse, Vivian. I know that's why you've come back to Nashville. Why else would you leave Mannheim's practice?"

"For your information, I outgrew Mannheim's practice. I wanted to branch out and expand my horizons further. Start my own trial, perhaps, and I couldn't do that in Munich."

"Why Nashville?"

"Why does it matter?" Vivian snapped. She didn't want him to know about her mother. No one needed to know that, but really if her mother hadn't been so sick she wouldn't have come back.

"It matters. So, why Nashville?"

"Why not?"

"Only because you were so hell-bent on leaving. You left like a thief in the night. I don't even remember getting to say goodbye. All I got was a note."

She saw the anger in him. The hurt. She couldn't blame him. She knew leaving like that would hurt him. It was a burden that she had to bear to protect herself.

The one time he'd really opened up ever, just after their first time, he said words which stuck with her to this day.

"I've lived a life of constant change. I want permanence. I want roots. Roots here in Nashville."

He wanted something she didn't and couldn't give him.

"I thought past was in the past? Focus on the now, remember?"

Reece stood up, his expression hard and cold. His jaw clenched tight. "Right. You're right."

"I'm sorry my coming back is hard on you, Dr. Castle,

but I'm here to stay and we have to work together so I suggest we make the best of it."

"Fine." Only she had a feeling it wasn't.

"Fine," she said.

"It's not like you'll be here that long anyways," he snapped.

"What's that supposed to mean?" It was like a slap to the face. Reminding her again that she'd left him behind, making her feel the guilt more keenly than ever.

Reece shrugged. "I mean once you don't get the job, Dr. Brigham's job, you'll leave."

"Who says I won't?"

"I wish I had your confidence, but you're going against tough competition. Old money, connections, things you don't have here." It was as if Reece was using all her old fears to scare her now. To get her to leave. Well, she was stronger now.

Vivian crossed her arms. "I've never been one to back down from a challenge. And even if I don't get it, who says I'll leave?"

Reece snorted. "You will. You'll move on to greener pastures. Isn't that what sharks do?"

The words haunted her because that was what Dr. Brigham had taught her. That was how she'd acted for so long as she'd fought to get surgeries as a resident.

"I'm not a shark."

Not anymore.

She cleared her throat. "I'm here to explore the potential of a trial on autism, if you must know. One I couldn't start in Germany. Just part of my working here was working with you on this case because I am one of the best diagnostician neurosurgeons in Europe, next to Mannheim."

He smirked. "So you're not after Dr. Brigham's job?"

Vivian shook her head. "Yes, I am. I have aspirations on Dr. Brigham's job. Who wouldn't?"

* * *

Me.

Only Reece kept that thought to himself. No one needed to know he had no desire or plans to run. He had no aspirations on Dr. Brigham's job. He preferred being on the front line. He liked the OR too much. He didn't like the spotlight or the PR aspects of running a surgical program. He didn't crave the spotlight like his parents did. Most people would think so, but he didn't. He abhorred it. That was why he didn't use his real surname. Why he'd changed Castille to Castle when he was eighteen. He wanted to hide the fact he was the son of country music royalty. He didn't want people to know that his father was Ray Castille, one of the biggest artists to grace the halls of the Grand Ole Opry. His mother, Edna, had been a model and preferred the jet-setting lifestyle and Hollywood over him and his father, to be honest. Wealth, fame and prestige destroyed lives.

Ruined people.

The limelight wasn't for him.

He hated the attention, the world he'd grown up in. Wealth and glamour did not lead to a normal childhood. So he avoided attention as much as he could. Privacy was what he wanted, though if his Alzheimer's trial was successful that could change. Bringing in money.

And maybe then he could help more people who couldn't afford health care or specialists.

Don't think about it.

"I'm sorry. Really, your reasons for returning aren't my concern. I was just… I was surprised to see you," Reece apologized.

She was going to say something more when his pager buzzed. It was a code blue on Gary. He turned on his heel and ran. He could hear Vivian following him.

"What is it?" she shouted behind him.

"Code blue," he shouted back over his shoulder.

As soon as he came into the room the nurse began to fill him in. It was a seizure, but one that seemed to be affecting Gary's heart as well. It was strange, both monitors showing his cardiac and neurological distress.

Vivian didn't ask any questions. She just dove right in, ordering medicine and keeping calm as she rapidly fired off instructions beside him. Just like the good old days.

"His pulse ox is down. He can't breathe," she shouted over the alarms. "Why is he not getting enough oxygen?"

I don't know. Only he didn't say that out loud as he pulled over the crash cart. They worked together over Gary like they'd worked together a long time ago. As if no time had passed at all.

He'd forgotten how calm and collected she was. How she grounded him. How she grounded the whole room in an emergency situation. He'd missed that.

"Charge to ten," she said above the din as Gary flat-lined.

Reece grabbed the paddles. "Clear." Everyone stepped back and he shocked Gary's heart back into rhythm.

The heartbeat stabilized, sinus rhythm returning and seizures ended. Reece breathed a sigh of relief as the monitors bleeped in time with a stable heart and his pulse ox rose again.

"Thanks," he said to Vivian. They shared a smile and it made his heart skip a beat because it was as if nothing had changed.

"No problem," she said. "That's what I'm here for."

He was glad she was here, but she'd left once. She'd leave again. He didn't need her. And he had to keep reminding himself of that to reinforce the walls he'd built.

"I can take it from here," he said, looking away quickly. Just working alongside her stirred so many memories within him. It reminded him of the hurt and pain from when she'd left. She'd been the one person he'd opened up to and she'd betrayed him. Broke his heart and just affirmed his belief that you couldn't trust anyone.

His parents and many so-called friends had shown him that. Even his parents had always been unreliable and never really there when he'd needed them. There was only one person Reece could rely on and that was himself.

"Are you sure?" Vivian asked. "I can stay…"

"No. Go get settled. I'll let you know when everything is set up to monitor him."

Vivian nodded and left the room, which he was thankful for. The last thing he needed was to carry on that heated conversation out in the open. One thing was for certain. He had to keep his distance from Vivian, which was going to be impossible to do, the longer Gary was in the hospital, but it had to be done.

For his own good.

CHAPTER THREE

"MAMA?" VIVIAN SET down her briefcase on the floor in the entranceway. She'd been surprised the door had been unlocked when she tried her key. Her mother never left the door unlocked, especially since they'd grown up in a less desirable location in the city. Although her mother's house wasn't in a bad part of town anymore; Vivian had taken care of that when she'd gone to Germany by buying this place. Still, it was no reason to leave her door unlocked.

The door being unlocked had Vivian on alert. Especially as there was no answer to her query when she first walked in. Her mother was definitely home as Vivian had the car now. Her mother's license had been revoked the day the diagnosis came down.

It didn't stop her mother from walking, though.

"Mama?" Vivian called out again, a little more urgent this time. She walked toward the kitchen and memories of that horrible day when she was a young girl came rushing back…the moment she'd found her mother in a pool of blood. Painful nightmarish memories that she hadn't thought about in a long time.

Her mother's suicide attempt after her father left was the stuff of nightmares for Vivian.

It was something they didn't talk about. That year, the year her mother checked out, haunted her for so long and in this moment, calling out to her mother, it was over-powering.

"Mama?"

Her mother rushed out of the kitchen, a tea towel in one hand, a dish in the other. She looked surprised. "Vivian? When did you get back?"

"Just now." She sent up a silent prayer of relief.

Her mother embraced her. "If I had known you were coming for a visit…"

Vivian's heart sank and she could see that faraway gaze in her mother's eyes. Her mother wasn't lucid. "Mama, I came home a week ago."

"What?"

"I moved back a week ago. Don't you remember?"

Her mother's eyes sparked and then there was recognition and the fog lifted. "Right. Oh, right. I remember."

"Do you?"

"Yes, yes I do." Her mother shook her head and laughed softly, obviously embarrassed and flustered. "How was your day at work? Back to your old stomping ground."

A nightmare.

Only she didn't say that out loud. She didn't want to upset her mother. Her mother knew about Reece and Vivian didn't want her to get the wrong idea about her return.

"Good. It was good. How was your day?"

Her mother sighed. "I thought it was good… I'm sorry to let you down. I swear I thought I was doing good."

"You're *not* letting me down and you *are* doing good. You just had a blip." Vivian ran her hand through her hair, trying to brush away the stress that was building. "How often do these blips happen, though?"

"I haven't had one since you arrived. At least I don't think so."

Vivian sighed again as her mother headed back into the kitchen. She'd been with her mother since she'd come home, but this was her first day away from her and she'd had a setback. Thankfully, nothing had happened, but perhaps she should look into having a nurse or a personal support worker here when she wasn't here. Just to help her mother with the blips. Although her mother wouldn't go for it.

"Don't go to all that trouble for me. I can take care of myself for now. You're here to work, not fuss over me."

Her mother came back and they settled in the cozy living room that was filled with overstuffed furniture, fake floral arrangements and pictures of her from her childhood. All the things that made her mother happy. Or so her mother said when she'd decorated the home. Either way, it was cozy and brought a smile to Vivian's face.

"So was Dr. Brigham excited to see you again?" her mother asked, excited.

"Yes, I suppose so."

Her mother smiled. "You suppose so? Well, I'm sure he was happy to see one of his students, one of his best students, back again."

"I'm not the only former student at the hospital."

"Oh?"

Vivian stopped herself because the last time she'd talked to her mother about Reece she'd told Vivian to break it off and never look back. Her mother had always stated Vivian had to be her own person. To put her career first and a man second.

"Don't give up on your dreams, Vivian. Not for Reece. I don't care if he's a good man or if you love him. You have to go to Germany. It's your dream. Go or you'll regret it."

Her mother had never approved of Reece. She'd thought he was a distraction and she'd been right. He was.

"Just some old friends. Old faces."

Liar.

Her mother smiled again. "Well, that's good."

Vivian nodded. "Yes. It's a big change from Germany, though. When I worked for Dr. Mannheim it was in a clinic. A private clinic. I'm not used to being back on rounds again."

"I'm sure you'll get used to it. Isn't it good to be home?"

"It's good to be home with you, Mama." Vivian glanced up into her mother's warm eyes. She did love being with her mother. She'd missed her while she was in Germany, but it had been hard growing up in Nashville. Even if they were far away from the kids who teased her, she would still wake up crying for a mother who wasn't there. Her mother had to work day and night to keep a roof over her head.

Nashville reminded her that love wasn't enough. Love made life harder. Everyone she loved left and she'd done her share of hurt too. Reece's behavior today was proof of that.

Even her mother was leaving. The disease was stealing her away, piece by piece. So young. Life was robbing her mother again.

"You okay, Vivian? Was it a rough day?" Her mother squeezed her knee. The blip was minor, but it was there.

"No, Mama. It wasn't a rough day."

"Good. You'll have to tell me all about it." Her mother got up and left, heading back into the kitchen.

Hiring a nurse, or at least a companion, would be top priority tomorrow. She'd call her mother's friend Florence to come sit with her tomorrow while she worked her shift at the hospital. It was too short notice to find a nurse now and Vivian wanted to interview people for the position.

Vivian would have taken the day off, but she'd only just started back at Cumberland Mills. She couldn't take the time off work. Especially not when she'd been assigned a high-profile case and was trying to vie for Dr. Brigham's position. If she took time off, it would not look good to those making the decision.

Reece had made it clear that he didn't think she had a chance at Dr. Brigham's job. Well, she'd prove him wrong like she'd always done.

There was a ping and she checked her phone. It was one of Reece's residents.

Gary Trainer was stable and talking. He'd also been cleared by cardio. The resident asked if she wanted to come by and set up the testing.

Vivian groaned. She did, but she also didn't want to leave her mother. If she told her about the text her mother would tell her to go.

Reece can handle it. Call him.

As much as it pained her to let go of the control, she owed it to her mother. She couldn't abandon her tonight. Vivian looked up Reece's number in the hospital directory and sent him a text. She didn't tell him much. She just mentioned that she was tied up for an appointment. No one needed to know her private life.

That was her business.

Fine, Reece texted back.

No questions—something she'd always liked about him. However, his shortness meant something different now; he was still angry at her. Vivian put her phone away and leaned back against the couch, exhaustion overtaking her. Maybe Reece was right and she was jet-lagged but, after a week, that seemed highly unlikely.

Sleep started to wash over her, warm like a cozy blanket.

A blood-curdling scream made her sit bolt upright and run to the kitchen. Her mother was on the floor, clenching her wrist, which she held up. Vivian had an instant flashback to the day after her dad left… No ten-year-old should have had to see that.

Snapping back to the present, Vivian rushed over to her mother.

"Mama!" Vivian knelt down next to her.

Her mother was in shock, shaking, eyes wild as she looked up at her. "Vivian? When did you get here?"

Reece cut through the emergency room. It was unusually calm tonight, which was never a good sign. Really he shouldn't even be down here, but it was the quickest way to the parking lot from where he'd been in the hospital. He hadn't planned on staying so late, but honestly there was nothing at home anyway.

He'd been surprised that Vivian had asked him to set up the monitors and get her test ready. It wasn't like her and he couldn't help but wonder what was wrong with her.

She's not your concern.

Still, it wasn't like her, but then what did he know? He clearly hadn't known her at all back then as he'd never thought she'd have been the person to leave him like she did.

"Can I have some help?"

Reece glanced up when he heard Vivian's stressed voice coming across the emergency room. She was holding up a woman, blood over them. And then his blood ran cold when he saw that the woman was Vivian's mother. He'd never told Vivian he'd met her mother; it had been brief, but that moment had been burned into his soul as the older woman had made it clear in a few words that she didn't approve of his relationship with her daughter.

"Don't tie her down, Dr. Castle. Let her soar. She deserves the chance."

He shook that memory from his mind.

And though he should let one of the ER doctors deal with it, it was instinct to help Vivian. He couldn't leave her like that. Reece ran over.

"Vivian?"

"Reece?" She shook her surprise away. "It's my mother. She had an accident."

He didn't say anything about knowing her. He just hoped Vivian's mother didn't recognize him. "Let's head over to the pod."

Vivian nodded and they guided her mother over to the room.

"What happened?" her mother asked, bewildered. "Where am I?"

"You're at the hospital, Mama. You had an accident in the kitchen."

"Oh," her mother whispered.

Vivian shot Reece a pained look and just in that quick moment he understood. He'd been studying the disease for so long he could recognize it easily. And then he knew why she'd come back to Nashville and it surprised him. When she'd left he'd thought she was selfish; maybe she wasn't after all?

"Mrs. Maguire, I'm Dr. Castle. I'm going to help you."

Vivian's mother nodded but she showed no sign she knew him. Reece examined the wound gently. It was deep and would need stitches.

"Do you need me to do anything?" Vivian asked. She was pleading and he understood the need to do something. He wouldn't be able to stand by and not do something.

"No, I'll take care of it. I'm going to sedate her, though. Is that okay?"

Vivian nodded. "It's for the best."

"Try and keep her calm." Reece grabbed the drugs out of the locked drawer. Vivian stroked her mother's hair and whispered to her gently. It took him off guard. He had never had that close relationship with his parents and never would. His father had died on stage, a lifetime of drinking and drugs having taken their toll on him.

His mother had died two years before his father's death. A car accident had taken her.

They hadn't been the best parents, and right now, watching Vivian, he was envious of what she had with her mother. It also made his heart melt a bit, seeing her so vulnerable.

Don't think about it.

"I'm going to give you something for the pain, Mrs. Maguire." Reece injected the sedative. "It'll help."

Vivian's mother nodded and then relaxed as she drifted off. Once she was out, Vivian started to help him as they inspected the deep laceration.

"How did this happen?" he asked as he began to repair it.

"In the kitchen with a knife, but I don't know why. She hasn't had violent tendencies." He could hear the anxiety in Vivian's voice. She was not telling him everything. Try as she might, he knew her, knew when she was lying to him, by the furrow of her brow and the fact she wouldn't make eye contact with him.

"What aren't you telling me?" he asked calmly.

"I told you all I know. I was in the other room," she snapped.

"Calm down," he said gently.

"You want me to calm down?"

"Look, I just think there's more to this than you're telling me. You're a horrible liar."

"Why do you think there's more to this?"

"There is a scar here, an old one," Reece remarked. "That's why I asked."

Vivian sighed. "It was a long time ago. I'm sorry. I don't like to talk about it."

"Right. I forgot you don't like to talk about the past."

"I'm not the only one."

He shot her a warning look, but she was right. "It's okay, Vivian."

"I didn't think… I mean. I don't know what I mean." There was a hint of sadness in her voice. Hopelessness when it came to this disease. He knew it well.

"When was she diagnosed?" Reece asked.

"Three months ago. Her doctor sent me the MRI. I finished up my affairs over there and headed here."

"I'm sorry." And he meant it. He wouldn't wish this disease on his worst enemy.

Vivian nodded. "Thanks, and I would appreciate you not saying too much about this. I like to keep my private life and work life separate. I don't care if people know she's my mother, just not why she's here."

"It's me, Vivian. I understand about that," he said gently.

"I appreciate it."

"Well, that explains why you were so interested in my Alzheimer's trial," Reece remarked. "Which makes me feel better."

"Did you honestly think I would try and poach that?" she asked, hurt in her voice.

"It's a tough world out there. Lots of people hungry for opportunity." Reece finished up his work. "You can't blame me for being suspicious."

"No, I guess I can't." Vivian handed him the scissors. "I'm not interested in Alzheimer's. That's not where I've focused my papers. I'm a diagnostician. Plain and simple."

"And you're here to diagnose Gary Trainer?"

"One of the reasons, though, truth be told, I didn't know about Gary until today."

They shared a smile—one he hadn't shared with her in so long. It was nice. He'd missed it. It was nice just knowing what another meant without having to explain. He disposed of the suture kit and then began to wrap her mother's wrist.

"Is this what had you tied up when you asked me to set up the test?" he asked.

Vivian nodded. "I couldn't leave her alone. I'm going to hire her a companion soon, but when I came home tonight she had left the door unlocked and had to be reminded about a few things. It was her first real bad day since I came home."

"I understand. I respect that."

He knew about bad days and parents.

His parents had been superstars and ran on a different schedule than the rest of the world. Reece had spent many a day sleeping during daylight hours and up all night, because that was what his parents did.

When he was a young child there were two years he didn't see the sun. Only the moon and countless strangers passing through their Belle Meade mansion while his parents threw endless parties and get-togethers.

How he'd wished for some stability.

A normal life.

The only stability he'd ever had in his life were the couple of summers he'd spent with his paternal grandfather in Kentucky, up in the mountains. There were regular meals, chores, swimming and stability.

Those summers had ended when he was ten, when his grandfather got Alzheimer's. Reece's father had sold the Kentucky cabin and put his grandfather in a home near Memphis, where he'd died alone a year later.

Reece had never seen his grandfather again. It was then he'd decided to dedicate his life to curing Alzheimer's.

That was all that mattered.

Medicine. Not music.

"She should be fine, but maybe try to find out if your mother tried to do harm to herself in her past. If she regresses it could be a repeat episode."

Vivian nodded. "I will. She doesn't talk much about those times. She's private too."

Reece chuckled with her. "I know, but I would hate to have to put her on a suicide watch."

"She's not suicidal when she's lucid," Vivian snapped defensively.

"Okay, but you understand where I'm coming from as her doctor."

"You're not her doctor."

"I will be."

Vivian looked confused. "What do you mean?"

Even though he shouldn't do it because it would mean that he would be further getting involved in Vivian's life, he couldn't see her suffer like this. Her mother was a good candidate anyway—given that Vivian had said she was early onset and was diagnosed only three months ago—and he had to keep telling himself that he was going to make the offer because it made sense for his trial…not because of his past with Vivian.

"I mean I've decided to take your mother in my trial."

Vivian was stunned. "What?"

"That's what you wanted, wasn't it? Your mother can start my Alzheimer's trial tomorrow."

This is not distancing yourself from her.

CHAPTER FOUR

"I THOUGHT YOU said your trial was full?" Vivian asked.

Reece shrugged. "There's room for a good candidate and I think your mother is a good fit."

"You don't have to make room for her because it's me." In fact she didn't want him to. She'd taken so much from him already. She didn't deserve this kindness and didn't want any handouts.

She didn't need them.

Except, her mother needed to be on his trial. It was a shot.

"I'm not. Don't mistake my offer for anything but the fact your mother is a good candidate." His eyes were dark, cold and it sent a shudder down her spine. "This has nothing to do with our past relationship. It's purely medical."

Vivian tried not to blush. Of course he wasn't doing it for any other reason and she felt foolish for saying it. What did she think—that he would still care for her seven years after breaking off their relationship with a note?

"Of course. I'm sorry. You don't deserve that. It's been a trying day."

His expression softened. "I'm sorry too."

"So why don't you tell me what you need for this trial?" Vivian asked, trying to steer the subject away from apologies for something that was no longer there. Something she never really deserved since she'd thrown it away.

"Well, first things first. I will get her admitted up into the neuro floor and we'll go from there." Reece turned to the computer and began to do the paperwork.

"Admit her?"

"Yes. All my trial patients are admitted until after I administer the medicine and they recover from the procedure so I can keep a close eye on the protocol. Will that be a problem?" Then he frowned. "I know you didn't want this spread around…"

"You're right, I didn't, but it's okay. She's more important. Besides, she has a different last name from me."

"Not Maguire?"

"No." And she didn't elaborate that her mother had kept Vivian's father's name, but Vivian had taken her mother's maiden name when she'd turned eighteen. She'd wanted to wipe her father's name from hers. She didn't need to be reminded she was the daughter of Hank Bowen, failed country singer, liar, cheat and drunk.

"So your mother's surname is…?"

"Bowen. Her name is Sandra Bowen." Vivian sighed and gave Reece the rest of the info he would need to admit her.

"Vivian?" her mother moaned as she woke up.

"Right here, Mama." Vivian gripped her hand and gave it a gentle squeeze.

"Where am I?"

"Cumberland Mills," Reece reminded her gently.

"Why?" Then her mother winced and looked at her bandaged wrist. "More than a blip?"

Vivian nodded. "Dr. Castle wants to admit you."

"I'm not suicidal," Sandra snapped. "Please believe me. The knife slipped."

It broke Vivian's heart because Reece had seen the old scars. Scars from a long time ago when her mother had been just that. Another reason why Vivian had wanted to sever the ties between her and her father.

"We know, Mama. It's not that at all…"

"I'm running an Alzheimer's trial. Your daughter, Dr. Maguire, will be helping and you're a perfect candidate, Mrs. Bowen." He smiled at her, one of those charming smiles which could win over any woman with a pulse and it worked like a charm on her mother.

"Oh, well, that sounds great. What's the trial testing?"

"Medication, Mrs. Bowen, that will hopefully cure Alzheimer's." He smiled again, but wouldn't look at Vivian. "I take it Vivian is your medical power of attorney now?"

"I am," Vivian said. Then she looked at her mother. "What do you say, Mama? Do you want to be part of the trial?"

"Of course." Her mother grinned. "Besides, I'll get to see you in action."

Reece smiled and patted her mother's arm. "That's the spirit. I'll get a porter to take you up to your room. Dr. Maguire, can I speak to you for a moment?"

"Sure." Vivian kissed her mother's head. "I'll just be a moment."

"Of course, darlin'."

Vivian shut the door to the trauma pod. "What do you need, Dr. Castle?"

"I just wanted to clarify something."

"Okay." Now she was confused. She thought everything was fine. Maybe he'd changed his mind.

"I said you were involved with the trial to ease her, but since you want her connection to you kept quiet you can't have any involvement."

"I assumed as much," she said, trying to not let her anger take over. Did he think she was so obtuse?

"I also want her MRI. The one her GP sent you."

"Of course. Anything else?"

Reece shrugged with indifference. "No, I'll update you as I know more."

"Okay. For what it's worth, thanks." She didn't wait for an answer. He'd made it quite clear why he was doing this for her mother. It was purely medical and she was fine with that. She expected that. Whatever they had in the past was long gone. And really all she wanted now for their working relationship was tolerance and professional indifference.

Reece regretted his demeanor toward Vivian the moment he uttered those words, but it was for the best. He knew bringing Vivian's mother on his trial was not going to distance himself from Vivian. Far from it. So he tried to delude himself. Tell himself the only reason he was doing it was because Vivian's mother was a perfect candidate for the trial. It had nothing to do with old feelings.

Keep telling yourself that.

It was hard to remind himself of that because every time he looked at Vivian he remembered every kiss, every touch.

The scent of her hair, the taste of her lips.

That was why he'd never had a long relationship after her. Vivian haunted him.

She'd taken his trust, something that was so hard for him to give, and crushed it. He knew he'd never feel that way again. Never open up again. So he didn't bother after a handful of bad dates and failed attempts at a relationship.

They always broke it off, saying he was never there.

And it was true.

His heart was in Germany.

I have to get away from here.

Reece turned and shut the door to the office. He was overtired and maudlin. Past was in the past. Focus on the now.

"Dr. Castle?" Reece turned to see one of his interns run toward him.

"Yes, Dr. Brody?"

Dr. Brody caught her breath. "Have you seen Dr. Maguire? She's needed in the ICU."

"Is it something I can help with?"

Dr. Brody shrugged. "I don't know. Dr. Brigham told me to find Dr. Maguire. He heard she had come back to the hospital and was in the ER."

Reece nodded. "I'll get her. Tell Dr. Brigham we'll meet him in the ICU."

Dr. Brody nodded and ran back the way she came.

So much for going home to have some sleep.

He didn't knock when he opened the trauma pod. "Dr. Maguire, you're wanted in the ICU. Dr. Brigham is specifically requesting you."

Vivian quickly looked down at her mother. There was such love and tenderness between them. Reece envied it. His parents had never shown much interest in him. Except when he'd walked away from the musical career they had wanted for him in order to go to medical school.

"You were invited to sing at the Opry. Singing at the Opry will launch your career. You can't say no."

"I can, Dad. I'm going to be a surgeon."

"You have a gift. You're throwing it all away."

"I have a gift, yes. A gift of medicine, Dad. I don't want a musical career. I don't want to be Ray Castille's son and always live in your shadow."

Reece had never wanted fame and fortune. Not in music anyway. He loved music, but he loved medicine and surgery more.

He wanted to be remembered for saving lives, not a gold record.

"Are you going to be okay, Mama?" Vivian asked.

"Sure. I'll be fine. Go do your job."

"I'll get a nurse to take her up to the neurosurgery floor and stay with her," he offered.

Vivian nodded and collected her things. They left the ER together after a nurse came to stay with Vivian's mother.

"I wonder what it's about. I'm not on duty."

"Someone saw you come in," Reece said.

Vivian sighed. "I guess it's to be expected, being the new kid on the block, right?"

"Probably." Reece held open a door for her.

"Weren't you on your way home?" Vivian asked.

"I was, but I want to get your mother settled first. Besides, I figured you'd want help navigating the maze of Cumberland Mills. It has been seven years. Things have changed."

She laughed. "Good point."

"Exactly. I'm always right." He winked.

"I remember the first time I tried to navigate these halls. I ended up in Pathology and missed my rounds."

Reece chuckled. "I forgot about that. First day of rounds too. Boy, was Brigham mad."

"You mean Isaac, don't you?" Vivian teased.

"I've never been able to bring myself to call him that." Reece held open the door for her. "He'll always be Brigham the blowhard to me."

She laughed, her eyes twinkling. "I forgot about that nickname. Seems so long ago."

"It was," he said and a blush crept up her neck. They didn't say anything else to each other then.

Dr. Brigham was waiting outside of an ICU room. "Ah, Dr. Maguire and Dr. Castle. Glad you're both here. We have a donor who was deemed brain-dead in the ER six hours ago, but an intern insists the patient was decerebrate upon a recent examination. Problem is she won't wake up on her own. She needs the ventilator to keep her alive. So all signs point to brain death."

"That's common," Vivian remarked.

"I know. So we did a scan and found a tumor. My question is, Dr. Maguire, can we get it out and if so will the patient come through? She was in a bad car accident. She survived surgery, but can she survive another one?"

"Can I see the scans?"

Dr. Brigham motioned for them to follow him into a room, where the patient's scans were brought up. Reece peered close. A routine scan in the ER had missed it, but it was there in the brain stem. A brain-stem glioma. Small, barely noticeable and a delicate place. If unsuccessful it would render the patient brain-dead.

"How did the ER doctor misdiagnose this woman as brain-dead? The glioma is preventing her from waking up," Vivian asked in disgust. "It's very rare and they're practically impossible to find at this stage. It's barely begun. I've removed two successfully. They weren't in adults and weren't this small."

"Do you think you can remove it?" Dr. Brigham asked.

"We'll tell the patient's next of kin the options. Send home the transplant team. They should never have been called in in the first place. She does have a shot and that's better than nothing."

"So glad you're here with us, Dr. Maguire." Dr. Brigham left the room.

"Do you think you can remove it?" Reece asked. He stepped closer to get a look at it. Dangerously close, so he took a step back, remembering she was off-limits. He'd forgotten himself for a moment there.

"I'll have a good shot. Frankly it's her only shot. This tumor will kill her eventually. Sooner rather than later. And she'll never come to in her present state with this tumor pressing here." Vivian sighed. "It's horrible, but whatever sent her to the ER might've saved her life. Do you want to scrub in with me?"

The question caught him off guard. He should say no, just go home for the evening after getting her mother settled, but this was a once-in-a-lifetime tumor.

"Yes. I would."

Vivian smiled. "Great. I need a surgeon I can trust in there with me."

He was shocked. "You trust me?"

"You're a fine surgeon, if my memory serves me correct. I need a good surgeon to help me. I don't know the other surgeons on this floor. I know you."

The compliment caught him off guard. "Okay. I'll get your mother settled and meet you in the scrub room."

She nodded and turned back to the scans as Reece left. He'd tried to push her away and the last place he wanted to be was in an OR with her for hours while they did brain surgery, but he wasn't going to walk away from a once-in-a-lifetime surgery.

He'd be a fool to turn his back on her and this opportunity.

And when it came to his career he was no fool.

Vivian hadn't felt this much pressure to perform a surgery since her first solo surgery. Funnily enough, Reece had been at her side then too. And she felt as nervous as she had that day long ago. Dr. Brigham had meant her first solo surgery as a test. She'd always been shy and quiet. He'd wanted to intimidate her. See if she'd crack under the pressure and quit the program.

And she almost had.

Except Reece whispered in her ear.

"You can do this. You're stronger than they think."
You can do this.

Dr. Brigham had been a little put out that she hadn't

asked him to join her, but she didn't want her old teacher breathing down her neck. When she got to Germany Dr. Mannheim had given her freedom and flexibility.

And with this surgery she needed to remain calm. Where she was working was a delicate part of the brain. One wrong move and the patient would be gone, but this was the patient's only chance.

It was also her first surgery back here at Cumberland Mills in front of her colleagues. Colleagues who were after the same position as her.

The pressure was on, to say the least. Which was why she'd chosen Reece. She needed him. Needed him to calm her down. Root her and keep her focused.

Reece walked into the scrub room in his blue-green scrubs, his scrub cap still the same from seven years ago. It was a piece of fabric with a forest in the fall. It reminded her of the trips she used to take with her mother—east to Knoxville or south to Chattanooga. They would drive through the Smoky Mountains. She loved it so much Reece once took her north to Kentucky. They'd spent the night in a cabin in the woods. Never once leaving the bed.

"We're the same," he had whispered against her neck as he'd spooned her in bed.

"No, we're not. We're decidedly different. And right now I'm extremely happy about that."

He had chuckled and run his hand over her bare shoulder. "I do like that difference, but that's not what I meant."

She'd rolled over to look at him, tucking her arms under her head. "I know what you meant."

"We grew up the same. Alone."

Emotions had washed over her and she'd tried not to cry. "We're not alone now."

"I know." And he had kissed her again.

She couldn't help but smile at the memory, but then her stomach twisted in a knot because that was long gone and she couldn't let her attraction for Reece interfere anymore. It was too dangerous. She was alone now.

Isn't that what you wanted?

"How's my mother?" Vivian asked. She needed to know that was at least taken care of.

"She's in her room and relaxing. The nurses and residents manning my trial patients will watch her. You don't have to worry."

"I do a bit."

"No one knows you're related to her. Just like you wanted." There was a hint of censure in his voice.

"What's with the attitude?" she asked.

"No attitude," he replied quickly, but he wouldn't look her in the eye. She wasn't an idiot. She knew he didn't approve.

"I don't want people to be sticking their noses where they don't belong. I don't care if it's found out she's my mother, I just don't want it announced and I don't want it to affect your trial either."

He looked at her then. His expression softened as he began to scrub in beside her. "I'm sorry."

"It's okay."

"No, I mean it, Vivian. I'm sorry. I naturally assumed… Well, forget what I assumed. Just accept my apologies."

Now she was intrigued. "What did you assume?"

"It doesn't matter."

"Yes it does!"

"I forgot how pushy you are." Then he grinned at her and she couldn't help but laugh with him.

"And I forgot what a stick-in-the-mud you can be. Now, tell me."

"Fine. Honestly, a lot of surgeons feel like family being sick in their workplace is a sign of weakness in them. They don't want others to know they are being affected personally."

"I can see that."

"And I assumed since you're going after Dr. Brigham's job that you would feel the same. I mean, you did your residency here, but you are technically new now. There are a lot of sharks out there vying for that position and I can tell you most of them are in the gallery to watch you remove this brain-stem glioma from the patient."

Vivian snorted and dried her hands with the paper towel. "Oh, I know. I'm used to living in a shark tank. My seven years in Germany have taught me how to deal with sharks."

His expression changed, his brow furrowed and the smile wasn't quite as sincere as it once was before.

"Well, I'm glad you know how to deal with it." He moved past her and headed into the OR.

Vivian frowned. One minute it felt as if no time had passed and then the next it felt that they were strangers.

You don't have time to think about it now.

And that was certainly true.

Right now she had to focus on this surgery, on saving this woman's life. She just hoped that whatever was bothering Reece wouldn't come up during the surgery because right now she had to depend on the man she'd known seven years ago. The surgeon who had been her partner.

The man she could depend on. The man she didn't deserve.

She took a deep breath and headed into the OR, where a scrub nurse helped her on with her gown and gloves.

"Where is the resident that noticed that she was decerebrate?" Vivian asked.

"She's in the gallery, Dr. Maguire," Reece said. "Dr. Berlin is the one who discovered it."

Vivian glanced up at the sharks. All the neurosurgeons were up there, scattered amongst the eager residents and interns who were there to learn. This was a once-in-a-life-time type of surgery.

She remembered seeing her first brain-stem glioma surgery, watching a seasoned surgeon do a delicate surgery to save a life, and what a rush it had been. That had been the moment she knew what her focus would be as a surgeon.

She wanted to work on the human brain.

It was also the moment she'd met Reece, because he'd been just as enthralled as she'd been watching that surgeon perform the surgery.

Vivian motioned and Dr. Brigham pushed the button for the intercom. "Is there something I can help you with, Dr. Maguire?"

She could see the more seasoned surgeons lean forward, anticipation on their faces, hoping that she would ask one of them to come down and help her.

"Can you send Dr. Berlin down? Ask her to scrub in. She's going to help Dr. Castle and I take out this beast."

"Are you sure you want Dr. Berlin?" Dr. Brigham asked skeptically. "I have assisted with this surgery before, Dr. Maguire."

"I know you have, Dr. Brigham, and I appreciate that, but I don't need another assist. Besides, Dr. Berlin is the one who questioned Dr. Low's diagnosis of brain death in the ER. Because of her we're here today and I would like her to join me."

"I'll send her down." Dr. Brigham motioned to the young resident in the front row. She could almost feel the glares, like knives jamming into her back, but Vivian didn't care. This was a teaching hospital.

She didn't need another head surgeon in her OR breathing down her neck, judging her. Frankly, she didn't need the resident in here either, but Dr. Berlin deserved to be here. Besides, if she did eventually get Dr. Brigham's job, smoothing the road between her and the residents and surgical interns wasn't a bad thing.

Vivian didn't have to be buddies with them. She wouldn't be, because then they'd never learn, but she wanted them to know that she was fair.

That she would give them a chance in the OR and that she could be a good teacher. And she was. She'd taught many German surgical interns. She'd been Dr. Mannheim's right-hand man in the last two years working there, so he'd given her the job of overseeing the education program as well as working on his various trials.

That was the key to becoming a successful Chief of Surgery as far as Vivian was concerned. As she glanced up into the gallery she could see that here at Cumberland Mills things had changed. It was a dog-eat-dog world.

"Where would you like me to shave?" Reece asked as he sat down at the patient's head.

"Just there over the base of the skull. You don't have to shave her entire head."

"Okay."

Reece began to prep the patient as Vivian went over her instrument trays. It was something she did a couple of times, silently to herself. Thinking about each instrument and the role they would play in the surgery. It helped her visualize it all.

She closed her eyes and thought back to the last one she did. It had been a bit different. The glioma was easier to visualize and this patient's was smaller. It would be no bigger than a strand of hair. So small and insignificant to the human eye, but deadly just the same. One wrong move and she could sever a nerve in her neck.

The brain was a beautiful thing in its intricacy and there was so much about it that they still didn't know. Especially when it came to things like autism, where people saw the world differently. And then there was Alzheimer's, which wiped away memories and processes until it eventually claimed the life.

Her mother didn't deserve to have Alzheimer's. It wasn't fair.

Everything I love is taken away from me. And I have no one else to blame except myself.

And as she watched Reece she thought of what she could've had with him. Only she didn't believe in that life. It had destroyed her mother. So losing Reece was her fault, but it was for the best.

Was it?

A lump formed in Vivian's throat and she pushed that thought away. She couldn't think about that now. She couldn't think of how empty her life was. Right now she wasn't a daughter; she wasn't hurting. Right now she was a surgeon.

A damn good surgeon.

"Dr. Maguire, I can't thank you enough."

Vivian's thoughts were interrupted by the eager resident who was getting gowned by the scrub nurse.

"Not at all, Dr. Berlin. I want to congratulate you on catching the subtle nuances of this. If it wasn't for you, our patient here would not have made it."

She might not even survive this.

No. The patient was going to survive this. She'd worked under a microscope of judging surgeons before. She could do it again.

She *would* do it again.

"Thank you, Dr. Maguire, all the same," Dr. Berlin gushed. And in the blush on Dr. Berlin's cheek Vivian saw a piece of herself. Who she used to be. Shy. Withdrawn. Never thought of twice and afraid to stand up.

"No more thanking. Go stand next to Dr. Castle and take a spot at the scope. You're going to get up close and personal with this glioma and the brain stem."

You can do this.

Vivian took another deep breath. She watched as Reece washed the newly shaved spot on the patient's head with betadine. The scrub nurse began to prep the surgical field as Vivian took her place as the head neurosurgeon.

"Scalpel." Vivian made the incision. She could hear Reece explaining the procedure to Dr. Berlin. She didn't even have to ask him; he just did it.

It was nice.

Why isn't he going for Dr. Brigham's job?

That she didn't understand, because he had the drive, he had the knowledge and the skill. He was a brilliant surgeon. Dr. Brigham's job was rightfully his. It should be his. Yet he showed no interest in it.

"I just want to focus on my Alzheimer's trial."

And maybe that was so, but Dr. Brigham had his own research going. It wasn't a one or another situation.

It's not your business. Don't get distracted. Stay focused.

Vivian had to keep reminding herself of that.

A life was in her hands.

CHAPTER FIVE

VIVIAN LEANED AGAINST the scrub sink, rolling her shoulders. The patient was in the ICU. She needed to heal. Her brain had swelled and Vivian would wait until the swelling went down to close up her work, but if all went well the woman should wake up.

Still, the next few hours would tell whether the patient would wake up or not.

And she planned to find an on-call room. As soon as she'd checked on her mother.

Right now, her body ached.

"You did good."

Vivian glanced over to see Reece standing outside of the scrub room. He'd left when the patient was wheeled off to the ICU while Vivian remained behind to dictate the OR report while it was still fresh in her mind. She liked the peace and quiet of the OR when everyone was gone. And his compliment made her heart flutter.

"Thanks. It was good to have you in there with me again. It was just like old times."

Reece shrugged. "Yeah, I guess."

"What time is it?"

"About four in the morning."

Vivian's shoulders slumped and she could feel the exhaustion washing through her. "I need to find a bed."

"Why don't you go home?" Reece suggested.

"Why? My next shift starts in about three hours."

He chuckled. "Oh. Mine starts in about two."

She groaned. "I'm so sorry for keeping you here. You were on the way out the door when we stumbled into the ER and ruined your night."

"It's okay. You didn't ruin it. Not completely." He winked and they shared a smile. "Besides, I haven't seen many brain-stem glioma surgeries here at Cumberland Mills."

"They don't show up very often in adults or caught at an early stage. Her family said she had no symptoms that usually appear when the glioma starts to strike. That car accident probably saved her life."

"That's for sure." He leaned against the doorjamb. "The last one I saw was the day we started dating and I haven't seen one since." She remembered that day. That day she'd stood up, spoken up just like Dr. Berlin did. That surgery gave her confidence that he always instilled in her.

It was also a rush. And that rush of surety had made her reach out for the thing she wanted the most and that was Reece.

She cleared her throat, trying not to think about kissing him now. "So one every seven years?"

"Something like that." He scrubbed a hand over his face. "I checked on your mother. She's sleeping but hasn't had a regression. We'll start the protocol later today. I'm sending her down for an updated MRI at ten, but I still need that previous MRI from you."

"Walk me to my office and I'll email it to you right now."

"If you're going to email the MRI why do I have to walk you?" he asked.

"Because I'm so tired I don't know how to get off the surgical floor. I don't want to end up in Pathology again."

They both laughed at that.

"Come on, then, pokey," he teased.

"Ugh, really. Even after all this time?"

Reece grinned. "Come on. When you're sleep deprived you turn into a sloth. That hasn't changed."

"You're a jerk," she teased back. "I haven't been on a hospital rotation in an eon."

"I know," he said quietly, pulling away from her again. Closing off.

"Have you checked on Mr. Trainer since he was hooked up for his testing yesterday evening?" Vivian asked, trying to change the subject and also stifle a yawn threatening to erupt.

"Yes, I did and so far no seizure activity."

Vivian cursed under her breath. "If he doesn't have any seizure activity in the next twenty-four hours and he's been cleared by cardio we're going to have to discharge him."

Reece nodded. "He's a bit antsy to go. He's singing at the Opry Friday night. Apparently, Thursday, two days from now, is rehearsal."

"So he won't voluntarily stay then if the test tomorrow comes back inconclusive?"

"No, he's pretty adamant to go." Reece sighed.

Vivian groaned. "I'll go see him."

"Get some sleep first. He can wait."

"I thought he was Dr. Brigham's VIP patient?" she asked.

Reece shrugged. "Yeah, but Dr. Brigham went home. He's probably sleeping and Gary is a decent person. He gets it. I told him you've been in the operating room since ten and you were catching forty winks. He understood."

"Are you sure?"

"What kind of patients are you used to working with?" he asked.

"Impatient ones." She smiled at him and stopped in front of her office. "Come on in and I'll send you the MRI."

Reece followed her in and she logged on to her computer and sent him the file. Then, all of a sudden, he was leaning over her. So close. He still smelled the same. That masculine scent which used to make her nervous and giddy at the same time.

Her pulse began to race at the thought of him so close. She was still attracted to him. That had never changed, and probably never would. Just being near him made her yearn for him again. She was weak when it came to him.

So weak.

He had been in the on-call room after surgery once, getting ready to sleep, when she snuck in and locked the door.

"What're you doing?" Reece had asked in surprise.

"Something I've wanted to do for a long time."

And then she had wrapped her arms around his neck and kissed him, trying to let him know how much she craved him in that moment. That she wanted him to be her first.

She wanted to be with him.

"Vivian," he'd whispered as he'd broken off the kiss. "What're you doing to me?"

"Kissing you."

Her courage had faltered, but when she'd reached up and kissed him again it had been the best thing she'd ever done. She'd wanted him. She'd just never known how to tell him.

"I know."

And then he'd cupped her face in his hands and pulled her into another kiss which had left her weak in the knees. And then, just like in one of those Hollywood moments, he had swept her off her feet and carried her over to the small cot, where the kissing had turned into frenzied lovemaking.

She'd pulled off her scrubs, not wanting to end their connection. All she'd wanted was to be naked with him. To have him possess her completely.

His lips had burned her flesh, making her cry out in heady pleasure...

"Can you bring it up for me?" he asked, interrupting her sinful thoughts.

"I just sent it to you." She fidgeted in her seat, completely aroused by that memory.

He frowned at her. "Just bring it up. Don't be so pedantic."

Vivian brought up the MRI and he leaned in closer. Her blood heated, her heart racing, and she tried not to think about what she'd just been thinking about because it all came rushing back to her right at this moment.

His hands on her. His kisses.

You broke his heart. You can't have him.

Only her body didn't care. She wanted him. Just as much as the first time—and that was the way it had always been when they were together.

"Yeah, looking at this, I can tell she's the perfect candidate for this trial. She's exactly what I'm looking for." Then he looked down at her and moved away from her fast, as if he was stung. "Thanks for sending that to me."

"No problem. You made room for my mom in the trial."

He nodded. "As I said..."

"I know, she's the perfect candidate," she said, finishing his sentence.

"Well, I have to start my rounds soon and I'm going to grab some coffee."

"Okay, I'll see Gary as soon as I catch some sleep and probably discharge him."

"All right. I'll see you later." Reece left and Vivian sank back in her chair. When she'd seen him again her heart had stood still, but being that close to him again... It was as if nothing had changed between them.

Except it had.

It was clear to her that he didn't feel anything for her anymore and really there was no one to blame but herself.

He managed to avoid her for twenty-four hours. Physically, that was, but he couldn't get Vivian out of his mind. Reece liked the floor in the early morning. It was quiet. He liked that sense of calm. He would like it even better if he hadn't been up for over forty-eight hours. It had been a long time since he'd pulled a shift like this. Not since his days as a resident.

That was when he didn't have an option to really have sleep. Residents and interns were expected to run every test, every chart. They were the last to sleep. Vivian and he used to hang out in the halls when it was quiet, chatting and drinking endless cups of coffee.

She had been his first true friend.

Growing up as the son of Ray Castille, there were plenty of people around; it was just none of them were genuine. Vivian had been genuine.

And then she'd become something more.

He'd opened up his guarded heart to her—something he'd never done with anyone—and then she'd left. She'd left for Germany and it had torn him apart. He'd bared his soul to her during their six months together. Told her his secret hopes for the future. Things that he'd thought she wanted as they both had hard childhoods. Only seeing her with her mother made him wonder if that was actually true.

Maybe he didn't know her after all. He'd never known her. Maybe they weren't the same.

He told himself that he wasn't going to get attached to her again, he'd keep his distance, but so far that was proving to be impossible. Especially when he worked with her in the OR. He'd forgotten how amazing they were together.

How in sync they were.

He'd let his guard down and fallen into an easy rapport

with her. To the point that when he'd been looking at the MRI he'd leaned over her. The scent of her shampoo was the same as it had always been. Coconut.

It reminded him of the first night they'd spent together and then the morning in the shower afterward.

Running his hands over her body.

He'd been her first. She had trusted him enough to let him be her first.

"I love you," he had whispered, overcome with everything he'd felt. Never wanting to leave the happy bubble of that moment.

She hadn't answered with words, but with a kiss.

At the time, he thought that the kiss was the same as the words he'd told her.

A kiss to say I love you.

How wrong he'd been. He'd given his heart to the wrong woman.

Don't think about it.

Why did she have to come back?

He'd gotten over her.

Actually, no. Who was he kidding? He was never over her. He'd just learned how to live without her.

Reece stopped in front of her office. The door was open but it was dark.

Just walk away.

Only he couldn't help himself. He peered inside and saw that she was lying on the couch in her office. Passed out. He could even hear her snoring.

It wasn't the kind of snoring that one might hear from a lumberjack. It was just a light gentle snore, one he was familiar with, and it made him chuckle softly because it hadn't changed at all. All those nights together. He'd never known peace like that since those summers in Kentucky at his grandpa's cabin. She moaned in her sleep and her brow furrowed. Reece smiled. He knew for a fact that those couches in Attending's offices were not comfortable at all. They were terrible, but after being up for forty-eight hours the couch in his office was looking mighty fine indeed.

"Dr. Castle, Gary Trainer's managers are on line three," Nurse Rodgers said from the charge station. "They want to speak to you and Dr. Maguire, but she's not answering her phone."

"Okay. I'll wake up Dr. Maguire and we'll take the call in her office."

Reece gently knocked on the door. "Vivian?"

She sat up. "What's wrong?"

"There's a call on line three about Gary Trainer. It's his management team and no doubt they want to know when we're going to release him."

"What day is it?"

"Thursday morning. His tests are done."

Vivian nodded and Reece answered the phone, putting it on speakerphone. "This is Dr. Castle and Dr. Maguire speaking."

"Yes, this is Buzz. Dr. Castle, I believe we've met, but I haven't had the pleasure of meeting Dr. Maguire yet."

"No, we haven't met," Vivian said, fighting back a yawn. "How can we help you?"

"I was talking to Gary two nights ago, before you hooked him up to the machines. There was an incident?"

"Yes, Mr. Trainer had a seizure and required a defibrillator to revive him."

"I know he wants out of there, but I can reschedule the Opry if you need to keep him," Buzz said.

"The problem, Buzz, is that he's checked out. He's been cleared by Cardio," Reece said.

"And Neuro?" Buzz asked.

"The tests came back inconclusive. He's doing fine and hasn't had a seizure since Tuesday," Reece stated. "His scans came back clean again. I don't think we can keep him at the moment and he's insisting that he doesn't miss his show at the Opry."

"When do you plan to discharge him?" Buzz asked.

"I want to run one more quick test and then I think by four in the afternoon," Vivian said.

"Okay, I'll send around a car for him. Thank you." Buzz ended the call and Reece disconnected Vivian's phone.

"You want to run one more test on him?" Reece asked. "When were you planning on discussing this with me?"

"As soon as I woke up." Vivian pulled her long red hair back into a ponytail. "Ugh, it feels like I got no sleep at all." She moaned and stretched her back.

Reece reached out instinctively and rubbed her back. "Those couches suck. You should've crashed in an on-call room."

"I intended to, but once I sat down I couldn't get back up." She stepped away from him. "Thanks, I think the kink's out."

"Sure." *What're you doing?* "So this test?"

"Something happened to Mr. Trainer on stage. He's been cleared of almost everything, yet when he took my hand when we first met there was weakness. Something is going on and I just want to run one more small test, a little scan before I let him go to sing at the Opry."

"But his seizures weren't induced by the bright lights or the loud music. We had him in a controlled environment for two days."

"Exactly. How controlled is an arena full of fans?"

Reece had to agree with her on that one. He remembered his father's last concert. The screams from the fans were almost deafening. There was no way to possibly mimic the sounds and the feelings of being out on stage.

If it was the concert in that huge arena that triggered Gary's seizures, at least the Opry was smaller and more intimate.

"Just one more test and if he passes we can discharge him," she said grudgingly.

"Well, that's if he agrees to it. When I checked on him thirty minutes ago he was chomping at the bit to leave. Why do you think Buzz is calling this early in the morning? I'm sure Gary was calling him to bring around his car."

"Has he performed at the Opry before?"

"Yes and there were no seizures."

Vivian bit her lip. "Yeah, but he's been singing for a couple years and in stadiums."

"I thought you didn't know who he was?" Reece teased.

"I did my homework last night." Vivian sighed. "He's quite a rising star. They say he's the next Ray Castille."

Reece's stomach knotted at the mention of his father's name.

Don't think about him.

"So what is the point you're trying to make?"

"I'm saying that he's been doing this for some time and never had a seizure before now. So what triggered these?"

"That's the question we're trying to answer."

Vivian didn't like the idea that they were letting Gary go. He was her first patient back at Cumberland Mills and Dr. Brigham had made such a fuss about him. When Reece and she walked up to his room, he was already up and about, back in his street clothes. When Vivian suggested another test he shot her right down.

"Look, I appreciate you two for saving my life, but I feel great. Perhaps it was stress related. I'm releasing an album later this week and I'm working hard for it to hit number one. The music industry isn't the same as it once was when the likes of Hank Williams and Cash were walking around Nashville. It's different. I've put in a lot of hours on social media and touring."

Vivian frowned. "If you think it's stress, then you need to take it easy."

Gary grinned at her. "I can't do that. As I said, I have an album dropping this week."

"Gary, we don't know what caused your seizures and that's troubling," Reece said. "What harm could come from running just one more test?"

Gary shook his head. "I appreciate it, Doc, I really do, but you had me hooked to those machines and I watched a flashing screen for hours and nothing happened. Nothing. I have to get back to work. I'm rested and I feel great."

Reece frowned at her. He was feeling the same way about Gary's discharge as she was. Gary might think he was fine, and medical evidence supported that he looked good, but there was something off.

There was something she couldn't put her finger on, but she was powerless. They couldn't keep a patient in the hospital against their will. Gary wanted to leave, so they had to let him go.

"Okay, if you're sure, Gary. If, however, you don't start to feel like yourself then you need to get back here as soon as possible so I can assess. You have to promise me." Vivian would've got it in writing if she could have.

"I have an idea. I'm singing at the Opry tomorrow night. Why don't you and Dr. Castle come, Dr. Maguire? That way you can be backstage and be on hand if something were to go amiss. Though I seriously doubt that."

"The Opry?" Reece tensed right up. There was an odd hitch to his voice. "You don't need us at the Opry."

Vivian shrugged. "I'm game. I'll go. I've never been to the Grand Ole Opry before."

"I thought I heard you were a Nashville native?" Gary asked skeptically.

"I am. I grew up on the east side of Nashville."

Gary winced. "That's a rough part of town."

"I don't live there anymore, thankfully, so yeah, I never did get to the Opry. I guess everyone from Nashville has to experience it once." Vivian looked over at Reece, but he wasn't making eye contact with either one of them. He looked upset. Bothered.

"Reece, are you okay?" Vivian asked.

Gary paused in his packing to look up. "Doc, you look like you've seen a ghost."

Reece scrubbed a hand over his face. "Nothing. Just tired. I still haven't had a chance to have a nap."

"Well, go have a nap, but promise me, Doc, that you'll be at the Opry." He looked at Vivian then. "That both of you will be there."

"Come on, Reece. It should be fun," she suggested.

"I'll think about it. If you'll excuse me." Reece left the room quickly without so much as a backward glance at them.

Vivian frowned and then she knew. It was because Gary had invited both her and Reece. Reece probably didn't want to go with her and that ticked her off. Not because he didn't want to go with her, but because he was ticked that they were invited together. Just because Gary had invited them both didn't mean Reece had to avoid it all together.

"I'll see you tomorrow night, Gary. Rest today."

"I will, Doc. Thanks."

Vivian left Gary's room and headed toward her office. She found Reece sitting in an on-call room with the door slightly ajar.

He shouldn't avoid the Opry because she was going to be there. He could go and she could go separately. Just because they shared the same patient didn't mean they had to travel together. He didn't even have to stand beside her backstage. He could pretend he didn't know her. He was acting childish.

She didn't even knock when she barged into the on-call room.

"Why don't you want to go to the Opry?"

"I'm trying to get some rest," he muttered.

"You didn't answer my question."

Reece sighed. "It's none of your business why I don't want to go. I just don't."

"It's because I'm going, isn't it?"

"Yes," Reece said quickly. "I don't want you to get the wrong idea if we went together."

"We don't have to go together," Vivian snapped. "Just because he invited us both doesn't mean we have to arrive together or even talk to each other there."

"Are you finished?" Reece asked.

"Yes, I think I am."

"Good. Close the door on your way out." He didn't say anything more to her. All he did was lie down on the bed, covering his eyes with his arm as if she wasn't even there.

His words stung, but what was she really expecting? So she shut the door behind her, trying to ignore the headache that was beginning to brew from lack of sleep, stress and frustration.

When it came to Reece Castle, she was going to have to keep reminding herself that she could no longer count on him for much of anything. Not even the benefit of the doubt. Whatever they'd had, even if in a brief moment they'd shared something, that something was gone.

CHAPTER SIX

"IT'S OKAY, MRS. BOWEN. You're okay. This is the MRI, remember?"

"Oh. Right. I'm sorry."

"It's okay. Just relax." Reece leaned back in his chair and the MRI tech started up the machine again. It was the second time that Vivian's mother had begun to fidget and forced them to stop the machine. She needed to be reminded of where she was, why her wrist was bandaged and where her child was.

She thought that Vivian was a little girl and she was calling for her constantly. Though Reece didn't imagine that being in the machine with a mask over her face would ease her anxiety.

Only Reece suspected it had more to do with the fact she was looking for her child. A mother who loved her child. He wouldn't know much about that...

He'd run away once. Hid in his tree fort for two days. No one had looked for him. No one had cared he was gone. When he'd gone back to the house, his parents acted as if he'd never left. They hadn't noticed his absence.

He was always an afterthought.

Vivian had told him she'd grown up alone like him, but he didn't believe it. Not now. Not now he'd seen the way that Vivian cared for her mother and the way Sandra obviously cared for her.

"Images are up, Doc," the MRI tech said.

Reece leaned over. "Damn. Can we get a deeper scan? Add some contrast."

The tech nodded. "Sure." And he got up to administer the gadolinium.

The Alzheimer's was progressing quickly and it was going to be hard to tell Vivian that. Even though she should understand logically, given the fact that she was a neurosurgeon as well, he found that when it came to themselves or their loved ones doctors were the worst patients. It was going to crush Vivian.

And after the way he'd treated her about the Opry invitation, he didn't want to be the further bearer of bad news. Besides, he should be here, working on his trial. Not gallivanting around Nashville.

Going with her to the Opry wasn't the reason why he didn't want to go. It was the fact that he would be recognized if he did go. His father's pictures lined the halls with the greats at the Grand Ole Opry. It was the Mecca to country music.

Everyone who was anyone in the country music scene was at the Opry on any given night and all of them would know exactly who he was—and he didn't like that one bit.

When Vivian had suggested she was the reason why he didn't want to go to the Opry he hadn't argued with her. He'd let her believe it and then he'd regretted it. He didn't really want to hurt her.

Even if when she'd first left all those years ago he'd thought about hurting her the same way she had hurt him, but that was when the wounds were still raw and he was younger. Watching her in the OR the other day had made him realize that she'd probably done the right thing going to Germany.

He didn't want to inflict pain on her, but he didn't want to tell her why he couldn't go to the Opry.

People in the medical circle didn't know him from Adam. He was just a damn good surgeon and he wanted to keep it that way.

Once Gary or Vivian learned whose son he was, they were going to look at him completely different.

Face your fear and go to the Opry. What can it hurt?

It had been a long time since he'd graced those hallowed halls. The last time had been when his father was alive and he was just about to go into medical school. His father was getting out on stage to sing for the first time since Reece's mother had died.

Reece had been so much younger then.

Maybe, just maybe, he could sneak in backstage and keep a low profile out of the spotlight. He didn't know of many hiding spots at the Opry. Too bad Gary's performance wasn't at the Ryman auditorium. He knew of plenty of hiding spaces at the Ryman. It was a place he would hang out while his parents performed, but the Opry rarely performed at the Ryman anymore. Not since it moved locations.

He'd liked the Ryman.

He'd liked running around the top level. The half circle, while his father did his sound checks and his mother ordered people around.

And there were fleeting times he'd imagined himself up on the Ryman stage. Singing like his father because, even though he had issues with his father and being Ray Castille's son, when his father walked out on stage he commanded a presence that not many people could imitate.

"Dr. Castle, Mrs. Bowen's scans are coming up again," the tech said, interrupting his thoughts. He hadn't noticed the tech had returned and administered the contrast.

"Thanks." He scrubbed a hand over his face. He had to get a control of himself, but since Vivian had walked back into his life memories were haunting him constantly.

The scans came up on the computer and Reece's heart sank. So much had changed from Mrs. Bowen's original MRI of just a couple of months ago. He had to start the protocol on her now or she would no longer be eligible for his trial.

Soon, whatever was left of Mrs. Bowen would be gone and it would invalidate the drug they were using.

"Where am I?" Mrs. Bowen's voice was shaking over the intercom.

"You're at Cumberland Mills, Mrs. Bowen. I'm Dr. Castle and we're doing an MRI. Do you remember?"

"Oh. Oh, yes. Now I do. I'm sorry."

"Don't be sorry," Reece said. He was just glad Sandra Bowen didn't remember him from seven years ago. The first time when she'd warned him off and the second time when she'd told him Vivian was gone and it was for the best.

"Am I done?"

"Yes. You're all done. Nurse Rose is going to take you back up to your room."

Reece sent the scans to his office. He had to find Vivian and get her permission to start as soon as possible. She hadn't signed the consent forms because they'd been so busy since her mother was first admitted. Now he had to track her down and get her to actually sign the forms. He wanted to start the protocol for his trial today.

As soon as he had the forms signed he would take Sandra into the OR and inject the medicine in a delicate procedure involving some nerves at the base of her skull.

He found Vivian in the cafeteria, nursing a large cup of coffee as she read a medical journal.

"Mind if I join you?"

She didn't look up from the medical journal she was reading. "Suit yourself."

"Is that in German?" he asked, craning his neck so he could see the words better.

"Yes, Dr. Mannheim's latest article. I like to keep up with his research."

"You didn't want to leave Germany, did you?"

"Do you want the honest answer?" she asked.

"Yeah, the truth, please."

"No, I didn't want to come back to Nashville. I didn't have the best childhood. Bad memories."

Bad memories was like a slap to the face. "I find that hard to believe."

"Why?" she asked, confused.

"I see the love between your mother and you."

Vivian's shoulders relaxed. "That's not what was bad. It was all the times my mother worked night shifts and I was home alone, scared. And then when my father left… my mother checked out. So my bad memories are tied to that. Nothing else."

Reece felt like a fool. "I'm sorry."

Then she reached out and touched his hand gently, her soft skin causing his blood to heat. Just the simple act of her touch made him want her. She affected him so deeply.

"You were never a bad memory, Reece. Never."

He moved his hand away, not letting her touch him. He wouldn't let her in again. He couldn't. Though in this moment he wanted to.

"I just got back from the MRI scan with your mother," he said, changing the subject.

She perked up then. "Oh, yes?"

"It's progressed since her original scan."

Vivian shoulders slumped in defeat and he couldn't blame her. "I figured as much. I didn't want to believe it, but…is she still eligible for the trial?"

"She is." Reece sat down and slid the papers toward her. "You need to sign the consent. I wasn't in a rush. I thought we'd have more time to get her wrist healed and run some more tests, but if you want her to stay on the trial I need to get her into the OR today."

Vivian pulled out a pen from her lab coat and signed the consent form. "How is she today?"

"The MRI was hard. I had to stop the test three times because she didn't know where she was and didn't seem to understand what year it was. She kept asking for her Vivi."

Vivian groaned. "Oh, that was her special little nickname for me. I hated it."

Reece chuckled and then took back the signed consent forms. He stood up. "Look, I'll be at the Opry tomorrow night."

"You will?"

He nodded. "Yeah. We have to keep an eye on Gary somehow."

She smiled. "We do."

He hesitated and he didn't know why. He had what he came for; he should just turn around and head back to Vivian's mother. Prep her for the injection.

"Do you want to come to the OR and be with your mother while I give her the protocol? It's a blind protocol. You would have to wait until I know whether she's getting placebo or the active medication."

Vivian nodded and handed him back the signed papers. "Sure, I'd like that. I'd like to be able to hold her hand. As long as it doesn't affect your trial."

"It won't. Not as long as you wait in the scrub room until the envelope is opened."

"Okay, I'll come down. When were you planning to take her down to the OR?"

"Now that I have your consent I'm going to head up to the floor and get her prepped and ready to go down. I have a small OR always on standby for my trial."

"Wow, that's very big of Dr. Brigham to grant you that." There was shock in her voice.

"Why are you so surprised by that?"

"Cumberland Mills is a large hospital that does a lot of surgeries. It's not specializing in just neurosurgery, where operating rooms can be kept on standby like that. Usually, things like trials have to wait until more emergent situations have the first go of it. I'm impressed. A lot has changed since I was here."

He was going to tell her that he was usually bumped when there were trauma cases, but he didn't have to because his pager went off and so did Vivian's.

"So, about that keeping an OR on standby, I think your mother's surgery is going to be pushed."

"Maybe not that much has changed." She stood. "I'll see you down in the ER."

Reece nodded. "Yeah, I'm going to get these consent forms up to my resident and I'll see you in five."

Every bone in Vivian's body ached. She'd been on duty now for days. She hadn't left the hospital since her mother had been admitted. And she hadn't wanted to go home, to be honest. Her shift wasn't over until four in the afternoon and, depending on the severity of the trauma rolling in, that could be pushed even further.

This was something she hadn't done in a long time and she hoped that she wasn't rusty. She stood at the edge of the ER. It was bustling as nurses and trauma physicians prepared for the incoming trauma. It was a multivehicle crash and there were several head and spine traumas and that was why she stood here with two other neurosurgeons, gowned and ready to take over as soon as the ambulances pulled up.

The air crackled with adrenaline. It was like standing at

the edge of battlefield or, as one author had once phrased it, *"The deep breath before the plunge."*

Reece came up beside her. "Gary is looking for us. We have to sign his discharge papers."

"Did a nurse tell him we'll be up as soon as this is over?"

"Yes, but that sometimes makes no difference to famous people." Reece sighed. "They don't like waiting."

"Well, he'll have to wait."

"What do we know so far?" Reece asked.

"Multivehicle crash on I-65. Lots of trauma, but I guess there was a couple not wearing seat belts who were ejected and have extensive head and back injuries."

He winced.

"We'll do this by teams of two," Dr. Brigham said as he walked up. "Dr. Castle and Dr. Maguire, since you're so comfortable working together, you'll work as a team and will take the female occupant of the vehicle."

She didn't really have much of a chance to argue as he moved down the line of other surgeons and began to delegate tasks.

"Whatever team is working on the female head trauma, her ambulance is pulling up," a harried nurse shouted above the din.

"Come on," Reece said as he took off at a jog toward the main doors. Vivian followed him. The blare of sirens was overwhelming and caused her heart to jump. When she'd been standing there and waiting for this moment she was afraid that she wouldn't remember what to do or how to act in a trauma situation. It had been seven years since she'd worked in an emergency room. Dr. Mannheim's clinic was for neurosurgery patients but not traumatic brain injuries right when they happened. Usually patients were brought in and they were stabilized.

Mostly, though, she removed tumors and honed her surgical skill as well as working in trials. Standing here outside of a hospital emergency room as an ambulance rolled up made her nervous. Only for a second, though. As soon as those doors opened it all came flooding back.

The paramedic jumped down and, with another paramedic, lifted the gurney.

"Patient, female, aged thirty, involved in a multivehicle crash. Was nonresponsive on the scene with a GSC score of three. Needed resuscitation at scene. Blunt trauma to the head and neck," the paramedic shouted over the din.

Vivian peered down as they raised the gurney and she took her spot beside it as they rolled the patient into the ER.

The wound on her head was packed, but she could tell it was extensive. There were contusions over her body and glass. The woman had gone through the windshield.

Why hadn't she been wearing a seat belt?

She let Reece guide them into a trauma pod, where they lifted her gently off the stretcher onto a hospital gurney. As the paramedics left to go back to the accident scene, Reece and Vivian began to work on the patient.

Instinct took over and she knew exactly what she was doing again as she began to cut away the bandages to reveal the damage that a plate of glass and twisted metal had caused.

"Does anyone know her name?" Reece shouted over his shoulder as he listened to her bilateral breath sounds.

"Carmen Sanchez," someone said, but Vivian didn't see who as she lifted Carmen's eyelids to check her pupillary reaction.

"Carmen?" Reece asked, leaning over as Vivian flashed a light. "Can you hear me?"

Vivian saw a reaction in the right pupil, but the left was not good.

"Left pupil is blown. We need to get her to CT." Vivian closed her eyes and checked on the laceration. "It's deep, but if we pack it we can get her to CT."

Reece nodded. "Breath sounds clear."

Vivian was amazed there wasn't more external damage. Of course that could be a totally different story when the scans came up. Having a Glasgow Coma Scale score of three wasn't good either and Vivian strongly suspected Carmen had an intracranial bleed.

"Let's get her down to CT," Reece shouted above the noise as he lifted the sides of the stretcher and Vivian made sure the IV bags and lines were secure.

"Ready?" he asked.

"Yep. You don't need to ask." They shared a smile.

Just like old times.

She followed his lead as they moved from the trauma pod down to the CT. Once again, no words were needed as they worked seamlessly together getting their patient into the CT and then watching silently as the images loaded onto the computer screen. She was holding her breath and praying for not too much damage.

"Intracranial hematoma," Reece remarked as the image came up. "Also bleeding in the abdomen. We need to page someone from general surgery."

"Yes. She needs to go into the OR now."

"I'll go get it prepped. You stay with the patient and page the general surgeon. You'll know the best one to work with."

"You know where the surgical floor is?"

"Yes, I swear I won't end up in Pathology again."

He chuckled. "Go. We'll be down soon."

She nodded and headed out of the CT room. Her body protested, but she ignored the exhaustion. She had a life to save.

Reece glanced at her as they worked on Carmen in the OR. The general surgery team was waiting until the craniotomy was finished before they went and assessed the bleeders. The bleeding from the spleen wasn't bad. The head had to be addressed first. As he watched Vivian briefly he could see the exhaustion on her face. Even though it was hidden behind a surgical mask, he knew the way she shifted her weight ever so slightly from foot to foot that she was tired.

Obviously, working in Germany had made her soft. Still, she was holding her own. He'd been worried that maybe she wouldn't be able to hold her own in a trauma situation, especially after being up for hours. He was pleasantly surprised, but he should've known. Vivian had always been driven. It was what he admired most about her.

It was why he'd fallen for her seven years ago.

It's why you still have feelings for her.

He shook those thoughts away and turned back to the craniotomy. He couldn't be thinking like that. Vivian was off-limits. He wouldn't ever put his heart on the line again for someone. He'd learned that lesson well.

"You okay, Dr. Castle?" It was so weird she was using the formal address. It was what he'd wanted when she'd returned and what was appropriate, given they were surrounded by nurses, other doctors and students.

It wasn't right to be calling each other by their first names.

He still hated it. It didn't feel right and that bothered him.

When she'd left he'd spent a year trying to forget her, to go on with his life. She had been back for a couple of days and already taking over his thoughts.

Focus.

"I'm fine, Dr. Maguire, and intracranial pressures are good."

"That's good. I think if she makes it through the night and through her splenectomy she'll make it. She's very lucky."

Reece nodded but didn't say anything as they worked together to evacuate the hematoma. He couldn't enter into a level of familiarity with her again. It would just set him up for hurt. Yet being so close to her, working with her, made him forget all the reasons why she was off-limits. Being with her felt right.

"So the Opry?" she asked.

He groaned. "Why?"

"What do you mean, why?"

"I mean why are you asking about it?"

She shrugged. "I don't know much about it."

"What do you want to know about it?" he asked cautiously. It was a subject he didn't like talking about. Especially not here. There was no place here in his life for a piece of his father's world.

"Why didn't you want to go?"

"No reason," Reece responded. "I really don't want to talk about it."

"Why?"

"It's private," he snapped, then sighed, annoyed with himself for getting snippy with her. "I'm focusing on the patient right now and not the Opry."

"So am I, but we used to chat like this all the time. Suction, please."

She was right. They did.

"That was a different time." Reece suctioned around the bleeder. "It's different now."

"Fine. I'll talk, then. It helps me focus."

"Suit yourself."

"To be honest, I'm not a big fan of country music."

There was a collective gasp. He was shocked, but then he remembered her saying it before. It hadn't bothered him back then. He had actually felt relieved. Less chance of her knowing who he was or, rather, who his *father* was. Reece was nobody and he liked it that way. Though his father had never been thrilled and he'd constantly reminded

Reece that he was a nobody because he was just a plain old surgeon.

Even though he'd hated his parents' lifestyle, he still loved the music. He still liked performing; he just liked medicine more.

"Not a fan of country? I'd honestly forgotten that. You know that's sacrilegious in Nashville?"

She chuckled. "I know, I know. My mother reminds me constantly about it. I'm a native of Nashville. I was born and raised here. I was also forced to watch endless hours of *Hee Haw* as a child."

Reece laughed. "Weren't we all?"

There was some laughter from others in the OR, people who'd grown up the same way as Vivian, but not him because he was pretty darn sure no one else had had the childhood he'd had.

Yeah, he'd watched *Hee Haw* and listened to the Opry on the radio but, more often than not, he'd been in the audience when his father was performing, feeling entirely alone.

"I just… I'm not a fan," Vivian said.

"That's too bad. Gary will be *so* disappointed," he teased.

She rolled her eyes. "I'll still go. Who knows, maybe I'll be swayed? I've been in Europe for a long time and maybe country music has changed."

"It's good, but it's still similar. Same themes."

"Oh. Great."

Reece chuckled. "Why don't I close up and you go discharge Gary? I'm sure he'll *love* to hear about your aversion to country music."

"Ha-ha." Vivian rolled her shoulders. "You sure you're okay?"

"Really? Come on."

"Sorry." Vivian stepped down from the microscope.

"You should be." Then he winked. "Go, and after you've discharged Gary, go home and sleep."

"What about that other procedure?"

He knew she was asking about her mother, but without announcing it to the rest of the staff. She wanted to be around for her mother and it just endeared her all the more to him. Of course she actually had a good mother. There had been a valid reason her mother had left her alone as a child. With his parents it had just been avarice and greed.

"Tomorrow. The ORs will be full tonight. As soon as one opens up, that procedure will be the next on the list and I'll make sure you're paged. Just go home and sleep while you can."

"Okay. Thanks." And she left the OR while he finished up the craniotomy so the general surgeons could get in there and start the repairs in Ms. Sanchez's abdomen.

It was good Vivian was out of the OR. This way he could collect his thoughts and not allow himself to continue to soften his defenses toward her, because the more time he spent with her, the more it was happening.

And that was a very bad thing.

CHAPTER SEVEN

"WATCH OUT!"

Vivian jumped out of the way as a roadie carrying an expensive-looking guitar pushed past her toward the stage.

So she stood off to the side and tried to stay out of the way. The backstage of the Opry was an overwhelming place for her. There were so many people and it was buzzing with activity. And of course she didn't know anyone from a hole in the ground. As she walked around there were pictures of all the greats of country music lining the walls. Those were the artists she recognized. Those were her father's idols. Cash, Hank Williams and Wynette.

One stood out and made her a bit angry looking at it. A picture of Ray Castille, who her father hero-worshipped.

Her father had wanted to be like Ray Castille to the point he'd neglected his wife and child to chase after that dream. Vivian resented Ray Castille. Which was foolish. Her father had never known him, as far as she knew. And, from what she'd heard about Ray Castille, he'd been a drinker and violent. Not the kind of person someone should idolize, but the man could sing like a siren.

"Why do you listen to his records? He's the reason why Daddy left!"

"You have to look past that, Vivian," her mother had argued. "You have to look at the music. Feel what he's trying to convey."

"How?"

And then her mother had got that wistful look on her face before she'd broken down sobbing.

Vivian sighed. Her mother had dreamed of being on the Opry stage; she might've become something if she'd been given the chance, but her father's jealousy quashed those dreams.

Sandra Bowen loved her husband so much that she'd do anything for him. Even end her career before it even started.

Now, standing here at the Opry, she resented her father for stealing this from her mother. He'd undermined her. Her mother should be here. Not her, because Vivian didn't appreciate it or understand it. Even when her mother pushed her as a young girl to sing. When her father left, Vivian stopped singing. She'd wanted nothing to do with this. Medicine was all she loved and all she could love.

And she didn't let any man get in the way of her dreams.

Yeah, but was it worth it?

Vivian stared up at Ray Castille's picture. There was something familiar about him. Something she couldn't quite put her finger on. Maybe it was just reminding her of all the times her and her mother were left alone.

"There is the most gorgeous doctor a guy could ever have," a sweet Southern drawl called out over the din of backstage.

Vivian turned around to see Gary walking toward her with the expensive guitar slung over his shoulder. Yesterday when she'd left the craniotomy to discharge him he hadn't been so charming. He didn't like to be kept waiting and he'd missed his sound check.

Of course he was remorseful when she told him about the accident and the fact she'd been in surgery. Now, backstage at the Grand Ole Opry, he was charming again. A totally different person. The person she'd first met.

His stage persona, obviously.

"Gary, you look great." That was a lie. One look at him had her concerned. Concealer couldn't hide the dark circles under his eyes, the yellow waxy tinge to his skin.

He nodded and tipped back his cowboy hat. "Thanks to you."

"I did nothing but write up your discharge papers." And now, looking at him, she wasn't sure if she should have.

"Exactly." He grinned again, flashing her those brilliant white teeth. "I see you found the hall of fame."

"Yes. Just looking at some names I recognize. My father was a big fan of country music."

That was an understatement. It had been his religion.

"Well, you should bring him here next time I perform. I'll get you tickets."

"Thanks. I'm sure he'd like that." It was a lie, but what else could she tell him? Gary was her patient and she wasn't about to spill her life story to him. She wasn't going to tell him she hadn't seen her father since she was ten.

"You do look fantastic tonight, Dr. Maguire. If you weren't my doctor…" He whistled.

Vivian just shook her head. "I am, though."

"Yes and that is a shame." He glanced over her shoulder. "Ah, and here comes my other fantastic doctor."

Vivian looked behind her and couldn't believe her eyes. She'd forgotten what Reece looked like out of his scrubs, but what was even more surprising was she'd never seen him wearing a cowboy hat. Ever.

It suited him.

He wore tight jeans and a gray V-neck shirt. Instead of cowboy boots he wore motorcycle boots. It all seemed to work and just from first glance she would've thought he was a country singer. It was almost as if he belonged backstage at the Opry.

Except for the fact he looked uncomfortable and stiff as

he approached them. His hands jammed deep in his pockets. Like one wrong move and he'd bolt.

"Dr. Castle, I'm glad you could make it." Gary stuck out his hand and Reece took it.

"Glad to be here, Gary." Only Vivian didn't believe him. There was something about what he said that didn't seem sincere. It was clear to her it was forced.

Tense.

It was clear to her he didn't want to be here, but why, since he'd been so vocal about the fact she'd said she didn't like country music?

"I didn't think you'd actually come, Dr. Castle," Gary said.

"Well, it was close." Reece glanced at her quickly. "Figured I better make an appearance once so you'd get off my back about it."

Gary laughed. "Well, I'm glad. I better get ready to go out on stage. See you both later at the after-party."

"After-party?" Vivian asked as Gary left.

"Always an after-party. They're not too bad. Just drinks, music and mingling," Reece explained.

"I'm not a mingler or a drinker. Especially with work the next day. Wait, how do you know what the after-party is like?"

"I've been to the Opry before. Remember, I do like country," he teased, relaxing.

She found that hard to believe, given the fact he seemed so uncomfortable. "Liking country and being backstage at the Opry aren't the same thing. Usually you have to know someone, or *be* someone, to get backstage."

"I think being at the Opry and liking country music is the same."

"You never told me you've been to the Opry before," Vivian said offhandedly.

"Does it matter?"

"You never spoke much about your past. Other than the fact you had a lonely childhood."

"I only talked about what I thought was important and this isn't. I attended the Opry and the after-parties a couple times before medical school."

"So who did you know back then to get backstage?" she asked, intrigued.

"You're full of questions lately," he said.

"I like to know who I'm up against."

"Up against?" he asked chuckling. "Are we in a competition, one I don't know about?"

"For Dr. Brigham's job."

He rolled his eyes. "I told you I'm not after his job."

"So you told me, but I don't believe it."

"Why? Why is it so hard to believe?"

Because you're talented. You're gifted and amazing.

"Because rightfully it should be yours. You're a damn fine surgeon."

It was apparent to her, her words shocked him, but he looked away, tensing up again as he crossed his arms.

"Thanks for saying that." Her compliment made him uncomfortable.

"It's just the truth. The job is yours. So take it."

"I'm not interested. As I've said before."

"That's a shame."

"Why do you want to talk me into competing for a job you're after too? Why is it so important to you?" he demanded. "If I wanted that job, it would be mine."

"You don't sound so sure."

He scrubbed a hand over his face, getting frustrated. "I'm done discussing this. I'm not after Brigham's job. I have no interest in competing. You need to let it go."

She knew she'd pushed him too far. "Fine. I won't bring it up again."

"Thank you."

"Let's welcome the Opry's own Gary Trainer to the stage!" The announcement came over the speakers backstage.

"I guess we better get somewhere to watch Gary," Vivian suggested.

"Yeah. Come on, let's get closer to the stage." Reece's hand touched the small of her back as he guided her through the small crowd gathered backstage.

Just a simple touch brought back so many memories. Of them dancing in the moonlight in the middle of Printer's Alley. His arms around her had made her feel so safe and so scared all at the same time...

"We shouldn't be here," she'd said nervously.

"Why not? This is a public place." Reece had begun to sway as he held her close. "We're not doing anyone any harm."

"It's midnight and we're standing in the middle of the street and it's snowing. Which is weird."

Reece had laughed. "It's a perfect time to dance. Besides, you said you always wanted to learn the two-step. Listen to the music coming from the bars."

They had stood there listening to the music and, before she'd had a chance to react, Reece had spun her around, making her shriek as he led her in a two-step. A quick dance to the rhythm of the music.

"Where did you learn to dance like this?" she'd asked.

Reece had chuckled. "Med school!"

She had rolled her eyes and then he'd spun her under his arm and brought her close, with that dangerous glint in his eyes that had made her melt like butter...

Vivian's heart fluttered as she stole a glance at Reece beside her, ushering her closer to the stage so they could see Gary walk out into the center, waving to a crowd of fans who were cheering and clapping.

She might have said she didn't know country music,

but she did. And as Gary stood out on that stage it made her stomach twist. It reminded her of hurt. Pain and of her father leaving. She'd been to a few concerts when she was young, but they were at smaller venues.

Her father never made it to the Opry. Her father never made it anywhere. And neither did her mother, but she could've.

There was a vibe in the air and it overwhelmed her with so many emotions Vivian thought were long gone and she shuddered. She was teetering somewhere between excitement and fear.

Even though the Opry wasn't like a stadium it was still the largest venue she'd ever been to and it thrilled her.

"Hey, you're Reece Castille, aren't you?"

Vivian turned to see an older man talking to Reece. *Reece Castille?*

"No," Reece said quickly. "No, sorry. I'm Mr. Trainer's doctor."

"Oh," the stranger said, crestfallen. "I thought you were for sure."

"It's okay. Happens all the time." Reece turned his back on the man, his face like thunder.

"What was that all about?" Vivian asked.

Reece didn't answer; he just shrugged. He couldn't even look her in the eye. He was lying, hiding something, and if Vivian didn't know any better she would swear she knew that man.

"I'd like to play you all a different song tonight, if I might? Tonight is the thirtieth anniversary of my idol's number one hit, *Only Hearts Are Broken*, and I want to sing you that song to honor the memory of Ray Castille."

Vivian winced. Her father would play that song over and over to her mother. And when he'd left, her mother would play that song over and over to remember.

Vivian hated that song. It reminded her of hurt, betrayal and shattered dreams.

It reminded her that she was no better than her father.

She wanted to leave but she was frozen to the spot when Gary turned and waved to them. "If it wasn't for my two doctors I wouldn't be here tonight. This song is also for them." Then the music started and Gary started singing the lyrics that still haunted her memories.

Leave.

"I can't stand here and listen to this." Reece cursed under his breath in disgust. "I've got to get out of here."

"Why?" she asked. "We can't both leave."

He looked confused. "Why do you want to leave?"

"Why do you?"

Before he could answer, though, the music cut off suddenly and there was a scream. They both turned in time to watch Gary's body jolt as if he was being electrocuted before his guitar crashed to the stage and his body followed after.

Vivian pushed past Security and ran out onto the Opry stage. Gary was seizing and Reece was beside her as they worked together to get him on his side. Reece was shouting off directions and demanding people call an ambulance. She tuned it all out as she pinned Gary's rigid arm to his side.

"Come on, Gary," she whispered, pleading with him to stay with her.

The seizures stopped, but then so did his heart. His ABCs were not good. Again he stopped breathing. Almost as if the singing had caused the seizure.

"Gary!" She rolled him back on his back and straddled his huge frame so she could administer CPR. She tilted his head back and checked his airways. "Gary. Come on, stay with me." She began humming the tune *Staying Alive* as she counted chest compressions.

"Drop the curtains!" someone shouted.

"Come on, Gary," Vivian said as she began to pump his chest. "Get me an AED!"

"Drop the curtains. You can't shock him on television," another person yelled.

"Forget about the damn curtains and get her an AED," Reece screamed.

Vivian tuned the world out but as she turned and looked at the audience one last time before the curtains dropped at the Opry, she saw her father's face looking up at her from the crowd.

Reece was glad to be leaving the Opry. He wasn't glad how it was happening, though. He'd rather sit through all his father's songs than have this happen to someone. The paramedics had arrived and Vivian was rattling off instructions as Reece helped them load an unconscious Gary onto a stretcher.

They'd got his heart to start again, but his blood pressure was not good and he hadn't gained consciousness. There was pupillary reaction but not much else and Reece had no doubt that if they hadn't been there Gary would've died on stage.

"Good thing we came tonight," Vivian said softly beside him.

"I was just thinking the same thing myself."

Vivian stood behind him and shivered. It was early summer, but it was still cool at night and all she was wearing was a sequined tank top, skinny jeans and open-toed heels. She looked so damn sexy, but she probably wasn't all that warm.

"Let's take my car and get to the hospital. Run some more tests," Reece offered.

"Sounds good."

He didn't have a coat on to offer her, so instead he

wrapped an arm around her, pulling her in close and holding her tight. It felt so good to hold her.

"What're you doing?" she asked, her voice trembling.

"You're shivering."

"Oh." She settled into him. It was nice, his arm around her as they walked toward his car. He wished it was a more leisurely stroll. He wished it was a different time. He wished there hadn't been any separation between them, but it was dangerous being so close to her. It made him forget the pain.

He couldn't let her get too close. It was bad enough that that producer backstage at the Opry had recognized him and she'd overheard. When he'd first seen her backstage she'd been staring at the picture of his father, frowning. He'd been so sure she was going to recognize him then, but thankfully she hadn't.

If she'd stayed in Nashville he would've eventually told her.

"Thanks for the arm. I didn't realize how cold I'd gotten. Sorry I freaked out."

"What did you think I was doing?" He opened the car door for her. "And I didn't think Germany was all that tropical."

She laughed uneasily. "It's not and I'm not sure what I thought. I'm out of sorts. Still in shock over what happened."

"You did good," he said as she slid into the passenger side.

"We both did," she said, but then she began to curse under her breath. "I wish we didn't have to let him go. I wish I knew what was plaguing him. It's driving me crazy that I can't find the cause."

"We'll find it."

What he didn't say was that he hoped it was before they were doing an autopsy. He wanted to find a cure for Gary.

"I know. I have to find it." She sighed. "I mean *we* have to find it."

He knew with that slip of the tongue that she was blaming herself, that she was putting so much pressure on herself. Even after all this time, her modus operandi hadn't changed.

So he didn't say anything else. If he did she'd push him away.

Isn't that what you want?

And that was something he couldn't answer.

CHAPTER EIGHT

"WHAT THE HECK HAPPENED?"

Vivian glanced back as she worked over Gary Trainer to see Dr. Brigham burst into the trauma pod, looking none too pleased. His face was red as he fumed. This was the Dr. Brigham Vivian remembered. As if it was her fault Gary had seized on stage. Dr. Brigham was two-faced enough to throw her under the bus if it came to it.

"Mr. Trainer had a seizure on the stage of the Grand Ole Opry," Vivian replied, turning back to Gary, who was unconscious. She had just made the choice to intubate him and put him in a medicated coma until she could figure out what was going on with him.

Every time he had a seizure his heart stopped, yet cardio had cleared him. It was a medical mystery, to be sure, and she didn't need to feel the added pressure of Dr. Brigham breathing down her neck, demanding answers.

She wanted to find out what was causing this in Gary. It was driving her crazy.

"Why was he discharged in the first place?" Brigham demanded.

"He was discharged because we couldn't find anything wrong with him and he passed a stress test. There was no reason to keep him," Reece snapped.

Great. Now Reece was fighting her battles. She didn't need him fighting her battles. It was bad enough he'd seen her at a weak moment backstage at the Opry. A moment made worse when she'd seen her father's face in the crowd as she'd worked over Gary. Only it couldn't have been her father. She hadn't seen him in many years but how much could he have changed, realistically—he couldn't afford the Opry. Not when he spent all his money on booze and goodness knows what else.

Taking care of her mother after her father left had taught her that she didn't need help fighting her battles. She could take care of herself. Besides, if Reece was fighting her battles, what kind of message would that convey?

It would tell Dr. Brigham that she couldn't handle this job, when she knew she could.

"Yes. Thank you, Dr. Castle. Dr. Brigham, legally, he had every right to leave. I gave him the facts and he decided to leave. Did you really want rumors flying that we unlawfully kept Gary Trainer locked up at Cumberland Mills?"

Dr. Brigham looked shocked but shut his mouth. It was obviously the right thing to say to get him off her back, but she knew she'd have to watch herself around him.

"Find out what's causing this," Dr. Brigham blustered and he left the trauma pod.

"You're doing the right thing," Reece said as he helped her intubate. It was as if he was reading her thoughts.

"I just wish I knew what was going on."

"You'll find out what's going on soon enough."

Vivian blushed. She didn't deserve Reece.

The intubation was finished and Gary was stabilized, even though he was in a medicated coma. She'd run some more tests and she'd stay as long as it took to find out what was causing his condition.

"We need to get him down to CT. I want a full body scan and I want some labs drawn. Get me a full array of blood."

"Yes, Dr. Maguire," the resident said. Vivian moved away from the bed and ignored Reece, moving past him. She needed to get into her scrubs and then she was going to head down to the research lab and start searching the neuroscience journals for something. Anything.

"You know, you'll never get Dr. Brigham's job if you snap at him," Reece said, falling into step beside her.

"Well, I had to let him know I could handle whatever he threw at me, especially when he's questioning my medical decisions. And I don't need you to stick up for me. I can handle my own battles."

He frowned. "Why are you getting angry at me?"

"I'm getting angry at you because he was talking to me. Not you. I can handle Dr. Brigham by myself."

"Fine. Handle him by yourself." Reece turned on his heel and walked the other way.

Vivian cursed under her breath, regretting her decision to snap at Reece. She always pushed people away because she didn't want to rely on anyone else. She only wanted to rely on herself. Her mistakes were just that and her wins were also hers as well.

Just keep walking.

Only she didn't listen to that inner voice. She ran after him.

"Reece, wait."

He stopped and looked annoyed with her. "What? Did I step on your toes again?"

"No. I'm sorry."

He cocked an eyebrow. "You've been saying that a lot recently."

"I know, I know. It's just I'm not used to this. I've forgotten."

"Forgotten what? Common courtesy?"

She rolled her eyes and then laughed. "Shut up."

He chuckled. "All right, all right, I accept your apology. I don't want you to beat me up in the hospital hall."

"Please. You know what I meant. I'm not used to dealing with politics and hierarchy like this. I'd forgotten how tough a teaching hospital can be. I'm used to doing what I want and when I want. I'm used to ORs being ready and I'm used to diagnosing patients a lot quicker than this."

It took a lot for her to admit that. Especially to Reece. He was a man she could somewhat trust, but not fully. He could still turn around and use that information against her to bring her down.

She knew how it worked.

"Your father loves us. He loves us, Vivian. You have to trust him not to hurt us. He'll come back for us, Vivian. He'll come back and take care of us."

The memory haunted her.

"I'm sorry you're so frustrated, but you'll find the answer." He didn't say *we* and that stung and she didn't know why. "I know it."

"Thank you for the vote of confidence. I don't deserve it."

He shrugged. "You're a good surgeon, Vivian."

"So are you."

Reece's face was unreadable. "Go to Gary and I'll page you when I take your mother down for her protocol."

"You're doing that tonight?"

He nodded. "She can't wait too much longer and the room is available tonight. I was going to tell you after the concert. Get you out of going to that party and mingling."

She smiled at him. "Thank you."

"Go get Gary dealt with. I'll wait until his scans come up before I take your mother down."

"Thanks."

He nodded. "Sure."

Vivian rubbed his arm. "Sorry for yelling at you."

"I'm used to it." He winked and smiled but she shrugged his hand off her and walked away. Vivian felt a bit better now that was settled. It put her at ease so that she'd be able to deal with Gary and his mystery illness, because that was the most pressing thing. His life hung in the balance, as did her career.

Only that wasn't as important as finding out what was attacking Gary and diagnosing him. Figuring out the mystery was why she'd become a doctor. It was what she loved to do.

She was going to discover what was ailing Gary Trainer and she was going to get him back on that stage at the Grand Ole Opry.

But first she needed to go to her office and get changed into her scrubs. Once she had tied back her hair and grabbed her identification she checked her pager to find a message from the resident saying they were just getting into CT scan.

So she had a few minutes.

She went to check on her mother.

When she peeked into the room, her mother was sitting up in bed and watching television.

"Mama, it's eleven at night. What're you still doing up? You need to get your rest."

Her mother looked at her. "Dr. Castle said that I was going down to the OR." She held up her hand to show her that she had an IV. "I haven't been able to eat or drink for the last couple of hours. He said he's going to take me after midnight."

"It's because you're getting general sedation. That way you don't feel anything when Dr. Castle gives you the medicine."

"*If* he gives me the medicine," her mother said. "It's a blind study. I could get the placebo, which sounds a bit like an amoeba."

Vivian laughed and squeezed her mother's hand. She was so glad her mother was lucid tonight and that they could chat like they used to. The only thing that would make this perfect was being back home in her mother's comfortable living room, or on the porch drinking sweet tea on a hot summer night.

"So where were you tonight?" her mother asked.

"Believe it or not, I was at the Grand Ole Opry."

"You're kidding?" Her face lit up.

"Not kidding."

"What was it like? I bet it was amazing. I always wanted to perform at the Opry." There was a wistfulness to her mother's voice which broke Vivian's heart.

"It was okay, but I was backstage for a patient."

"So you were there when Gary Trainer collapsed?"

"I was. I administered CPR to him. He's my patient."

"Wow. I can't believe that." Sandra smiled and leaned back against her pillows. "So unbelievable."

"Why?" Vivian asked. "I'm a neurosurgeon."

"I know, darlin', it's just that I still see you like that little baby I brought home from the hospital."

Vivian laughed. "That reminds me, stop telling Dr. Castle stories about me."

"He's cute," Sandra said.

"Mama, you know who Reece is, don't you?"

Her mother nodded. "I know. I may not have known before, but I put two and two together. You did the right thing going to Germany. You advanced your career. Now you're the doctor to Gary Trainer and spending nights at the Grand Ole Opry."

"My job's not all that glamorous," Vivian teased.

"Don't burst my bubble, Vivi."

Vivian shook her head and laughed. "I'll try not to."

"So what happens now?"

"What do you mean?" she asked. "Between Dr. Castle and me?"

"No, I mean with me."

Vivian let out a sigh of relief because she wasn't sure she could answer her mother or whether her mother would accept any answer she gave. "I'm going to head down to Radiology and check on my patient. I just want you to know I'll be in the OR with you. You won't know it, but I'll be there holding your hand when you're under and I'll be here when you wake up." She leaned over and kissed her mother on the top of her head. "Good night, Mama. Stay out of trouble."

She headed down to Radiology and got there just in time for the scans to come up on the computer. The brain was clean; there were no lesions.

Nothing.

Damn.

She scrubbed a hand over her face. She needed time to think. "Email me the scans and take Mr. Trainer up to the ICU. Monitor him closely and if there's any change, any little blip, page me. I'll be in my office."

"Yes, Dr. Maguire," the resident said.

She was going to find out what was ailing Gary Trainer if it was the last thing she ever did.

"Dr. Castle, it's the active ingredient," his resident said as he showed him the vial containing the drug and not the placebo.

Reece smiled behind his surgical mask and nodded. "Thank you."

He took the syringe and held it, ready to inject it.

"You can let Dr. Maguire in now."

"Yes, doctor." One of the nurses headed into the scrub room and brought out Vivian.

"You can take her hand, Dr. Maguire."

Vivian grinned from behind her mask. "Thank you, Dr. Castle."

He nodded. "Injecting the protocol." He peered in the microscope and watched as the active ingredient worked its way into Sandra's brain. They had to wait a few moments for it to work before they could finish up and revive Sandra.

He smiled as he glanced over at Vivian, holding her mother's hand. There was such a tender love there. Something he'd never experienced. He was envious of the connection she had with her mother because it was what he'd always wanted.

There were times he'd wondered if his parents even wanted him, let alone loved him.

He wasn't so sure, since he'd disappointed his father so much by heading to medical school instead of singing.

"You're nothing."

And the thing was, sometimes he really believed it. He'd really believed he was nothing when Vivian had left all those years ago and then again when his father had died and there was so much left unsaid.

So much he had wanted to say, but it was too late.

His father had died while on stage and Reece was busy during medical school. He'd barely made it in time for the funeral and when he had refused to sing his father's songs he'd managed to upset what little extended family he had left.

Maybe I should have sung.

The guilt still ate away at him.

"How did it go?" Vivian asked, glancing over his shoulder.

"Beautifully," Reece said.

"Thank you."

"It's my job." And that was the truth, but also he was

happy to do it for her. She had such a hold on him. "Okay, well, let's get her up to Recovery."

Vivian leaned over and kissed her mother's forehead through her surgical mask, while Reece finished.

He walked out of the OR with Vivian. "You know everyone knows what your mother is in here for, right?" Reece asked.

"I know. It was mostly the wrist injury I wanted to keep hidden. If everyone knowing she's my mother means she gets treatment that may help her, then I don't care if they know my business at this point. My mother is more important."

"How were Gary's scans?" he asked, trying to get his mind off what he'd just witnessed in the OR and to get his thoughts off his father.

"Clean."

"Clean?" he asked in disbelief. "How can they be clean?"

She shrugged. "I'm about to hit the research lab. I plan to read every darn medical journal about strange neuroscience I can get. There has to be something. It's almost like Parkinson's, yet it's not."

"You'll find it. I have faith."

"You're supposed to be my partner in this, or have you forgotten?" she asked. "You can come to the research lab too, you know."

Reece laughed. "I haven't forgotten, but your specialty is diagnosing the mysterious. The ball is in your court."

"Thanks. I think."

"You'll do well. Your mother will be in Recovery for a couple hours and the protocol does have a side effect of migraines so she's going to be kept pretty much sedated until the morning. So go work. Figure it out."

"And where will you be?" she asked.

"What does it matter?"

"I guess it was my roundabout way of asking whether or not you wanted to come dive into back issues of neuroscience magazines and medical journals. You were always good at the research."

He wanted to do it. He really did, and he wasn't doing anything now except an OR report. Only he couldn't. He had to keep his distance from her.

"I would love to, but I have rounds."

He could see the disappointment in her eyes, briefly. "Sure. Well, thanks again for taking such good care of my mother."

"It was my pleasure. You'll figure out Gary's medical mystery, I have no doubt."

"I plan to. I'll see you around." Vivian left the scrub room and he cursed under his breath. It was for the best.

At least that was what he kept trying to tell himself.

CHAPTER NINE

VIVIAN HAD BEEN stuck in that lab for two days. Or at least it felt like it. Gary's condition had stabilized and he was no longer in a medicated coma. He was disoriented and the weakness in his hands was continuing.

The spinal tap came back clear. As with every other test.

All she could do right now was keep Gary in the hospital and under constant supervision. She ran between Gary and her mother's rooms. While she did that she read every neuroscience magazine that she could and she knew that the other neurosurgeons were beginning to question her ability as a diagnostician.

She heard the gossip. Caught the pointed stares and heard the whispers.

Her career at Cumberland Mills was riding on this.

This was why she was brought in, because she was one of the best in diagnosing and solving perplexing medical mysteries that revolved around the brain. She was positive the answer was under her nose, she just couldn't see it.

The only one who didn't question her abilities was Reece.

He was the only one who had encouraged her, who was kind to her when she clearly didn't deserve that from him. Not after what had happened in the past. Why did he have to be so nice and caring? Why did he have to take care of her mother so well?

Why did he have to be such a damn good surgeon?

And why did he want to be her friend? She didn't deserve it.

She didn't want it.

Yes, you do.

"I don't normally say this, Dr. Maguire, but you look awful," Gary said weakly from his bed. "You look stressed."

"You're one to talk," she teased.

He smiled weakly at her. "You need to get out of this hospital."

"I'm not the only one." She finished her charting. "How are you doing?"

"Tired. I want out of here too."

Vivian's heart sank. "I know. I'm working on that."

"I was supposed to sing at the Red Swallow Bistro down in Printer's Alley tonight. I got someone else to do it for me—why don't you go there and have a drink on me? I'll be fine."

"No, I'll stay close by."

"I know you're off duty, Doc. I asked. Go. It might help refresh your brain too. I have a private table at the Red Swallow. It's a nice quiet booth. You can have a drink and enjoy some music. Maybe a change of scenery will help you figure out what's wrong with me."

"Did Dr. Castle tell you I'm not a fan of country music?" she asked suspiciously.

Gary grinned. "He did."

"Is that why you're pushing this on me?"

"I am. I aim to change your mind yet." He winced. "Come on, Doc, humor me."

"I don't think that will work." Though she was sorely tempted to get out of the hospital, going back to her mother's house was no better. It was so lonely there. Maybe she should take Gary up on his offer and go somewhere where no one knew her.

Where no one would be questioning her skills and whispering about how she was a failure.

"Come on, Doc. Just go check out my replacement. It would put me at ease. You know, less stress."

Vivian rolled her eyes and then laughed. "You're terrible."

He grinned again. "I know it."

She sighed. "Printer's Alley?"

"It's not far from here and, besides, the walk will do you good. It'll clear your mind."

"I know where Printer's Alley is. I'm from here."

"Good, then you know exactly how far it is."

"I'm not going."

She had spent so many nights in Printer's Alley with Reece. Huddled together in a secluded booth having a coffee, talking about medicine or not talking at all. And there had been the time in the winter, when a rare snow had begun to fall early in the season, catching them off guard...

"It's starting to snow." Vivian had stood there, staring up at the inky-black sky. "I've never seen it snow this early on."

Reece had stepped out the door of the bistro and stared up at the sky. "Must be El Niño."

She had snorted and then laughed. "I can't remember the last time I really watched it snow."

"It snows every year," Reece had said.

"Yeah, I know, but I can't remember the last time I did this—you know?" She had held up her arms and spun around.

"What? Dancing in the snow?"

"No." She'd stuck out her tongue and caught a snowflake.

"Haven't you heard about acid rain?" Reece had teased.

"You're a stick-in-the-mud."

"Oh, *am* I?"

Then he had pulled her close and begun to sway.

"Let's dance, then. That's what I like to do in the snow…"

"So what's the holdup, Doc? Why won't you do this one favor for me?" Gary pleaded again, interrupting her thoughts.

"Fine, but you need to rest for the rest of the night. No television. Sleep."

"Deal, but when you get back I want a report."

"Fine, but if you're asleep I'm not going to wake you."

"Get out of here, Dr. Maguire," Gary said, laughing, and then laid on his Southern accent really thick. "Go on, now—git."

She didn't really want to go to Printer's Alley to watch Gary's replacement at a bistro, but maybe a change of scene would do her some good. She changed into her street clothes and decided to take the short walk to the bistro.

It was still early in the evening, but late enough that the sun had set. She could see the pedestrian bridge lit up against the dark night. Usually the streets were quieter in the fall, but it was summer and there were a lot of tourists milling about. They were being brought in by shuttles from various hotels to the normal tourist traps.

The Red Swallow Bistro wouldn't be on their radar.

Which was good. If she had to endure a night of live country music, she wanted it to be in a relatively peaceful place so she could think.

"Can I help you?" the hostess asked as soon as she walked in.

"Yes, Gary Trainer sent me over."

"Oh, yes. You must be Dr. Maguire. Gary called me and let me know you were coming," she said sweetly. "Follow me."

Vivian followed her through the darkened bistro that

had white Christmas lights strung from the low rafters. The mood was definitely intimate and rustic.

"Here's Mr. Trainer's booth. Can I get you a drink?"

"A sweet tea with something in it would be nice."

The waitress smiled. "Sure, I'll be right back."

Vivian slid into the booth, which was off to the side and in the shadows. You could see the stage area. The entertainment hadn't started for the evening. The small stage was lit up with a circle of light and on the wall behind it were various neon signs and signed country music paraphernalia.

The rest of the bistro was wood, brick and stone. It just gave off a rustic feel. That was the best way she could describe it. Vivian relaxed against the plush leather seat in the booth. It had been so long since she'd really relaxed like this.

Seven years was too long.

"Here you go," the waitress said, setting the tea down. "Mr. Trainer said your drinks are on the house."

"He doesn't have to do that. I can pay for my own drinks."

The waitress shrugged. "He insisted and, since he owns most of the shares in this place, I'm not going to argue with my boss."

Vivian chuckled. "Fair enough. Thank you. When does the live music start?"

"Soon. If there's anything else you need, just holler."

"I will."

The waitress left and Vivian took a sip of her spiked sweet tea. The alcohol went straight to her head and though she wasn't sure what they'd put into her tea she didn't care. It tasted great.

"Ladies and gentlemen, we have a very special guest with us here tonight. He's a close personal friend of Gary

Trainer, who is still in hospital, so please give a warm welcome to Reece Castle."

Vivian almost choked on her sweet tea as Reece came out of the shadows of the stage, a guitar slung around him and his black cowboy hat down low. Reece? He was Gary's special guest? She knew Reece could sing but why he would agree to it? He hated the spotlight, but it was him. He walked across the stage, keeping his head down as he sat on a stool. The house band came out and sat behind him. Another guitar, an autoharp player, percussion; it was a bit surreal for her.

"Thank y'all for having me here tonight. I thought I would sing some songs that mean a lot to me and Mr. Trainer to let him know we're thinking about him tonight."

Vivian watched with bated breath as he began to play the guitar and the lyrics of the song Gary had been singing a few nights ago, Ray Castille's song *Only Hearts Are Broken*, slipping from his lips, but what made a shiver race down her spine was that she heard Ray's voice in Reece. Which was eerie since Ray Castille had been dead for a long time, but it was as if he was in the room. She'd heard Reece sing before, but never really listened. It was eerie, hearing him sing like this. She'd never put two and two together before now.

And she wasn't crazy, as a few people around her began to gasp and whisper, but only for a few moments as they sat back and listened. Reece had the audience under his spell, as if he was weaving words which held them captive and enthralled.

Something she'd never seen him able to do.

He moved so quietly through the halls of Cumberland Mills. Almost like a shadow. He didn't speak out or step out of line. Most people thought he was harmless and didn't think twice about him, but she knew better. Vivian knew that he didn't take guff from anyone and he was fiercely talented.

Here, though, he had a commanding presence.

With his voice he reached out to the audience and ensnared them, holding them captive. It was mesmerizing and she was just as captivated as the rest of the audience. Just as spellbound. And when his performance finally came to an end there was a standing ovation, which she joined in.

And it was then that he saw her. Their gazes locked across the bistro and she couldn't tell whether he was happy to see her or not, but he didn't take his eyes off her...

"Now that you've taught me to two-step, what're you going to teach me next?" she had teased as she'd run her fingers through the hair at the nape of his neck.

"I thought I would sing for you."

"Sing now?"

"Yep."

And then he'd begun to sing in her ear. A sultry song she hadn't recognized, but she hadn't cared because it had been the man singing it to her, holding her close on that snow-covered street in the middle of the night that had mattered...

The song ended and there was applause. She was breathless, her heart fluttering at the memory. She'd been so in love with Reece it was overwhelming, all the memories coming back to her.

I should leave.

"Thank you, everyone. Have a good night," Reece quickly said before disappearing off the stage.

Vivian sat back, suddenly nervous, and she didn't know why.

It wasn't long before Reece made his way through the crowd, but he was no longer the country singer. He was the man she was familiar with. He slid into the booth, his back to the stage.

"I'm surprised to see you here," he said.

"I could say the same of you."

He nodded. "Well, it's a side of me that… I can't even finish that sentence."

"Why?"

"Singing in public is hard for me. It brings back too many painful memories."

At least that explained his behavior at the Opry.

"I didn't know you performed like this."

"I don't."

"You're amazing. In fact you sound exactly like Ray Castille. I've never noticed it before. It's eerie."

His look was thunderous; even in the shadows she could see the change. "How do you know Ray Castille's music? I thought you hated country music."

"I grew up listening to it. He was my father's favorite. He wanted to be like him."

Reece nodded slowly. "I don't sound like Ray Castille."

"You do. It's uncanny and I'm not the only one who thinks that way. You should've seen the audience, their faces when you began to sing. It was… I can't describe it."

Reece shook his head. "You're wrong."

"No, I'm not." Then she reached out and touched his hand. "Why does it bother you so much? You have a talent."

He stiffened. "My talent is surgery."

"Yes, that too, but singing… It was beautiful. It was better than Ray Castille as far as I'm concerned."

"No, Dad was the far superior singer."

Reece watched her closely. It didn't take her long to process what he'd said. It was a shock to him that he was actually admitting it. That he was telling someone that his father was Ray Castille. That he was finally telling Vivian his darkest secret.

That he was the son of a late country music legend.

A son who'd done nothing but disappoint his father by walking away from the gift of music to pursue the gift of healing instead.

"You can heal souls with music, Reece. You can't with medicine."

Telling her, though, felt like a weight was lifted off his shoulders. He'd been hiding this from her for so long. It felt good, but also made him nervous. Why was he letting her in like this?

And for a moment he regretted his decision.

"Your father?" Vivian stammered. "But your name…"

"I changed it."

She blushed. "You have me there. Why did you change your name, though? You're country music royalty."

"No," Reece snapped. "I'm not. I'm a surgeon. I love music, but it's not my passion. Medicine is."

She nodded. "I get that. Does Gary know who your father is? Is that why he asked you?"

"No. He doesn't know. He knows I sing. He's caught me at some smaller venues and he's been asking me to come here and perform for a long time, but my schedule doesn't let me."

"For someone who is vehemently against connections to one of the greats, it's so odd that you come out here and sing."

"I'm not vehemently against it. Music relaxes me, but I'm careful about it. I don't perform often and I avoid the places where people might recognize me. As you said, my father was a country music star and there were a lot of parties. It's why I changed my name. I just want to keep my anonymity."

"Fair enough. Though singing your dad's stuff and sounding like him, it will be hard to keep that secret."

"I have been able to keep it secret for most of my life."

"You got me there." She smiled at him and it made his heart skip a beat. He liked seeing her like this, relaxed and talking with him as if no time had passed. "I never noticed it before. I can't believe I haven't."

"It only seems to come out when I sing his stuff. I never sang his songs to you before."

She smiled. "True."

"I'd appreciate it if you didn't tell Gary about this, though," Reece said. "Or he'll bug me to perform again."

"I won't tell him, but you know word is going to get out. You're skating on thin ice, my friend."

"What will they hear? That there's a guy who can sing like Ray Castille? As long as they don't know the real truth it doesn't matter."

"And you don't think Gary is going to ask you to sing with him at the Opry, especially if you sound like your dad, which you do?"

"Well, my schedule just became impossible. He'll forget about it the longer I put him off. Like most music stars I've had the acquaintance of, he'll move on to something new and shiny in no time."

"How is your trial coming?" Vivian asked. "I know you don't like me asking about it, but I'm curious."

"It's coming along well. The medicine is being well received." And it was. All his patients were doing well and Sandra was recovering nicely, with only a few minor side effects.

"Have you been to see your mother since she came out of sedation?"

"I have and she hasn't had too many blips. When will you release her?"

"By the end of the week. I have a few more memory tests to run on her." The waitress set down a cup of coffee in front of Reece.

"Can I have a coffee, maybe with a shot of espresso?" Vivian asked.

"Sure," the waitress said, taking away the empty glass that had been sitting in front of her.

"Are you planning on burning the midnight oil?" Reece asked.

"Yes. Until I find out what's causing Gary's illness."

"You'll find it."

"Why do you have so much faith in me? I mean, it's clear the rest of the hospital is questioning my abilities, but you have faith in me. Why?"

Because I've never lost faith in you, even after you destroyed me.

"You're a good surgeon."

"Excuse me, Mr. Castille."

The voice addressing him by his family name sent a shiver down Reece's spine. He turned and saw an older man in a bolo tie and suede jacket standing beside the booth—the one who had approached him at the Opry.

He'd recognized the man too, but couldn't place him then. Now he could. Andrew Sampson. His father's producer and the man who'd written several of his father's platinum hits, including the one he'd sung tonight.

"I'm Dr. Castle. Not Mr. Castille." Reece didn't like lying, but telling Vivian was one thing, letting the whole world know was another.

The man smiled indulgently. "If you say so. But you can't deny how much you sound like Ray."

"Thank you," Reece said quickly. "This is Dr. Vivian Maguire. She's working with me. We're both treating Gary Trainer at Cumberland Mills."

"A pleasure to meet you, Dr. Maguire."

"Thank you, Mr. Sampson." Vivian then slid out of the booth. "I really have to head back to the hospital. I'll let you two gentlemen chat."

Reece got up and touched her elbow. "You don't have to leave."

I want you to stay. Don't leave me here. He needed her, but he couldn't vocalize those words. He couldn't ask her for that.

"No, it's okay. I'll get my coffee to go and head back to the hospital. I won't feel good until I figure out what's wrong with Gary. I'll see you later at the hospital?"

Reece nodded. "Yeah."

He watched her leave and his heart sank in disappointment. He was trapped and now he really regretted coming up here and singing his father's songs, but tonight he'd been feeling maudlin. Watching Vivian with her mother made him yearn for something he'd never had with his parents. Tonight he'd been regretting not seeing his father more often, for not working out his issues with him.

So he'd broken with tradition and sang his father's songs.

He shouldn't have done it.

"You're a doctor now?" Andrew asked as Reece returned to the booth.

Reece nodded. "I am. I'm a neurosurgeon."

Andrew's eyebrows raised. "I'm impressed. I always knew you were bright."

Reece cocked his head to one side, giving up on trying to pretend he wasn't Ray Castille's son now that the two men were alone. He snorted. "Did you?"

"Of course." Andrew cleared his throat. "So you and that pretty doctor are treating Gary Trainer?"

"Yes."

"I hope Gary recovers soon. What's wrong with him? There's a lot of talk."

"I'm not at liberty to say. I can say the talk is wrong."

Andrew smiled. "Well, it's great to hear that the gossip is just that. It's always so disappointing when talented musicians fall prey to the drink and drugs."

A knot twisted in Reece's stomach.

"How can I help you, Mr. Sampson?" Reece asked, shutting those memories of his parents' past from his head.

"The thirtieth anniversary of your father's first single going platinum is coming up. It's sad he's not here to celebrate it with us at the Opry, but you have his gift, son. Come sing at the Opry. Come sing for your father."

Sing for your father.

Only he couldn't.

Singing at these small venues was one thing, but getting up there on the stage and singing for all those people... He couldn't do that.

He was a nothing.

"I'm sorry, Mr. Sampson, but I'm going to have to decline. My work just won't allow me to do it. I'm sorry, but I have to get back to the hospital."

He didn't stick around to listen to all the reasons he should sing for his father's big anniversary. He wasn't sure if he could do his father justice anyway. It made him angry at himself, at his father. This situation was the exact reason why he didn't want people to know who he was.

What he'd done was foolish.

Just one night and he was standing in his father's shadow. He was no longer Dr. Reece Castle. He was Reece Castille, son of Ray Castille, and he would never measure up to his father's greatness.

He collected his guitar and went out the back of the bistro into the alley, keeping his hat low so that no one would notice him.

"Where you headed, cowboy?"

Reece was startled to see Vivian standing in the shadows. "What're you doing here? I thought you were going back to the hospital."

"I was, but then when I got halfway there I remembered the way your face looked and thought I should return. You okay?"

I'm fine.

"I wanted you to stay."

"And now?" she asked.

Leave.

He should tell her to go home. He should go home.

"I want you to stay."

A blush crept up her cheeks. "Good."

"Want to get out of here?" he asked.

"More than anything."

He took her hand. "Let's go."

And he knew the moment he took her hand in his all bets were off and all those walls he'd built up to protect himself from her were threatening to come down and he didn't care.

Not one bit.

CHAPTER TEN

VIVIAN HAD NO idea where he was taking her, but they were leaving Nashville behind them and she suddenly realized that they were heading out of town toward the woods northeast of the city.

"Where are we going?" she finally asked. "You're not taking me back to Kentucky, are you?"

"Kentucky?" he asked, confused.

"Don't you remember that cabin in the woods?" And the night they'd spent wrapped in each other's arms.

"Oh." His expression changed and he cleared his throat. "No, we're not going up to the Smoky Mountains."

"Are you taking me out to the woods to murder me now that I know your secret?" she joked, trying to ease the tension.

"No." He looked at her as if she was crazy.

"Don't look at me like that. You're the one being mysterious."

"You want to know where we're going?"

"Yes."

"My cabin up in Hendersonville."

"Your cabin?"

"Yeah, I bought it five years ago and restored some of it myself. It borders Johnny Cash's land—well, not his land anymore."

Vivian cocked an eyebrow. "You have hidden depths."

"Cash is my favorite singer."

"Not your father?" she asked.

"No," Reece said quickly. "If you don't mind, I don't want to talk about him. I've had enough of talking about him tonight."

"Sure thing." She understood that. She didn't like talking about her father either. It made sense why she and Reece had connected right from the get-go. She'd never known why, but hadn't questioned it.

They'd had so many good times together and worked well together. Reece had been her closest and best friend, but it was apparent she'd never really known him. Not at all. Just like he hadn't really known her.

No one really did and it was better that way because she didn't deserve to have anything more than what she had right now and she wasn't sure she could trust anyone with her heart. Not after watching her mother's heart break over and over again through the years.

He turned down a wooded path that was switchbacks through the woods until they came to a small clearing, where a cabin was lit up. As if expecting someone to come. She realized it was more than just a cabin he visited occasionally. This was his home.

"You live here?"

"I do."

"I thought you'd live in the city. Maybe in your family home."

Reece snorted. "It's a shrine to my father now. Sorry, a *museum*. I prefer this. My grandfather had a place like this. I spent many a happy summer here, until he passed from Alzheimer's."

"Well, now I know why your focus has been on that."

He nodded. "I loved my grandfather. He led a simple, humble life I appreciated and one I wasn't exposed to very often."

He parked the truck and Vivian stepped outside and stared up at the night sky. She could see the stars without the light pollution from the city. It was beautiful. She could hear the gentle lapping of water against the shore. It reminded her of that Kentucky cabin and it made her heart skip a beat, remembering what had happened there.

Even though she hadn't wanted anything more than a fling, that cabin in Kentucky was the place where she'd lost her heart. Where their six-month relationship had started. She'd never told him that, though; she'd kept that to herself. She couldn't help but wonder when he'd bought this place, but she didn't want to know the answer.

It would just remind her of the pain she'd caused him. Of the love she had never deserved to have.

"Feel like a marshmallow?" Reece asked, intruding in her thoughts.

Vivian chuckled, the silly question shaking away all those guilt-ridden thoughts. "How random. I can honestly say that I've never been asked that before. Are you offering me a marshmallow?"

Reece grinned. "I am. I was thinking about having a fire and roasting a couple."

"Well, I'm going to pass on the marshmallow, but a fire sounds heavenly."

He shrugged. "Suit yourself, but you don't know what you're missing. The best thing in the word is a burnt marshmallow."

Vivian laughed out loud. "I forgot about your affinity for well-done food."

"Except steak. Can't stand a dry steak."

She took his hand as he led her out back to where his fire pit was. The lake was shimmering in the moonlight and there were fireflies dancing at the shoreline and through the low boughs of the pine needles.

Before her father had become obsessed with being a

country music star there had been a few times when he took her fishing in the moonlight. It was one of those halcyon memories that she held dear and it hurt to think about it right now.

There was a crackling sound as Reece brought the fire to life. She turned and took a seat on one of the benches surrounding the fire pit. It was cushioned and had a high back, so she could lean against it.

Reece was crouched by the fire, feeding it kindling, his cowboy hat pushed back.

"It suits you, you know. Can't remember if I told you that."

"What does?" he asked.

"The hat. I never saw you wear one before. I like it. You look so mysterious." Then she blushed, realizing what she'd said.

He smiled but didn't look at her. "Not the scrub cap?"

"No, I didn't say that. I like the scrub cap too. I always have."

"Good, because the scrub cap is the preferred hat."

"I know," she whispered. "I haven't been to the lake in ages."

"You used to come to the lake?"

"Yes, with my father." Then she cursed under her breath for mentioning her father. For letting him intrude on this moment. "He used to bring me here when I was very young. I haven't been up here in a long time."

"You don't talk about your father."

"Neither do you," she whispered.

"True." He stood up and took a seat beside her. "Your mother talks about him."

"Does she?" Vivian's spine stiffened and her stomach twisted in a knot. "What does she say?"

"She loved him and he left."

"That's pretty much it in a nutshell." Vivian relaxed. "He broke her heart."

"And what about your heart?" he asked, his voice soft and gentle.

"Yes. Mine too." She choked back the emotion threatening to bubble up inside of her.

Why did he have to be so kind to her? She didn't deserve his care and concern.

"How is your heart now?" he asked, prying a little too deeply for her comfort.

"My heart is fine."

Liar.

He nodded, but she could tell that he wasn't convinced. "How about those marshmallows now?"

Reece got up and walked into the house. Vivian sighed. What was she doing here? She should just call a cab and head back to the hospital. She shouldn't be here, alone with Reece. He was dangerous to her.

He reminded her of all the things she couldn't have.

Of the things she didn't deserve. She wouldn't hurt him again because she couldn't promise him any kind of future.

She stood and made her mind up to leave when Reece came back outside, carrying a bag of marshmallows and a guitar bag.

"What're you doing?" he asked, watching her inch away from the fire.

"I think I should go."

"Why?"

"I think it would be for the best."

"I think you need to sit down," Reece said sternly. "Besides, a cab won't come out this far this late at night so you're trapped and totally at my mercy."

"At your mercy?"

"Yes. I'm going to force you to eat a marshmallow." He winked.

Vivian rolled her eyes but sat back down. The fire was warm and it felt good. "So what's the guitar bag for?"

"Believe it or not, it has a guitar in it." He was teasing her. Just like he used to do. It was nice.

"I know that."

"I was going to sing," Reece said. "Your mom said you sing too."

"What?" She shook her head. "I don't sing. So put it away."

Reece shrugged. "It's something I do out here."

"I suddenly feel like I'm in a John Denver special," Vivian muttered under her breath.

Reece tipped back his hat and laughed. It had been a long time since she'd really seen him laugh like that. It made her heart melt just a bit and all those good times came rushing back. Endless nights on night shift and laughing together down a darkened hallway over something completely ridiculous, but when one was sleep-deprived it was the funniest thing in creation. It was a shared joke like that which had ended with her in his arms for the first time.

She'd been laughing so hard and had been so tired that she'd tripped and he'd reached out for her, bringing her tightly against him. When she'd looked up into his eyes, suddenly it hadn't been all that funny anymore and she'd been swept away in a passionate kiss.

The only man who'd even been able to make her feel that way. She'd kissed other men after Reece, but none compared to him. None.

And just recalling that moment made her cheeks heat, a shiver of anticipation racing down her spine.

"So what're you going to sing for me?" she asked, trying to knock those dangerous thoughts from her mind because if she kept lingering on those delicious memories she was apt to forget herself and throw herself in his arms.

Her heart couldn't take his rejection.

"I think we'll sing my dad's song, 'Under My Spell.' Do you know it?"

"Yes," Vivian said. "I know it, but I'm not going to sing."

"Why?"

"I don't sing, but I'll listen." She would gladly listen to him sing again, even though letting him seduce her with his music was probably not a good idea.

Reece began to pick at his guitar, the familiar melody of that lonesome love song—one her father had been good at mimicking—floating out across the darkness. It had been her favorite song, but her father had ruined that.

Still, with Reece singing it, it made her forget her father.

It made her forget everything and before she knew what she was doing she was singing along with him to the words she thought she'd forgotten but were somehow still there. She couldn't help herself. She'd forgotten how much she used to love to sing. Especially with her mother and father.

That was before her father had left. When her childhood had been somewhat happy.

Sort of normal.

That was why she hadn't sung for so long. It was too painful, but singing with Reece felt right. It felt as if they'd been doing it for a long time.

Their gazes met across the fire and it was as if an invisible tether reached out and bound them together in a shared moment, their voices melding and meshing together perfectly in sync. It made goose bumps rise on her arms. It carried her away.

And when the song ended, the magic didn't. His eyes were sparkling in the firelight, her heart was pounding in her ears, her pulse racing.

Run. If you know what's good for you. Run.

Only she couldn't run. She didn't want to run.

Before she knew what was happening he was setting

down his guitar and closing the gap between them. His hands were cupping her face, his fingers brushing the nape of her neck, and then his lips were on hers.

Kissing her, making her melt into his arms in a heady rush of pleasure. And she knew without a doubt that this kiss was not enough; she wanted more.

She wanted his hands on her body, touching her places that no one else had touched. She wanted him again. She wanted him pressed against her, making love to her, but she couldn't have that.

She didn't deserve that.

Vivian pushed him away, placing her hands on his chest. She could feel his heart was racing like hers.

"I think I should go home now," she whispered, her voice hitching in her throat because her body was protesting.

"I think that's a good idea," Reece agreed huskily. He took a step back from her. "Just let me put out the fire and I'll meet you at the truck."

Vivian nodded and walked toward the front of the house, the spell broken. She glanced back to watch him throw sand on the fire, breaking up the logs so it wouldn't keep smoldering, and she wished there was some way to stop the fire that was burning for him inside her.

But when it came to him, she knew it wasn't a fire that could be easily extinguished.

Reece wasn't sure what he'd been thinking last night. He hadn't planned for that to happen; he hadn't wanted it to happen. Last night was just supposed to be a friendly campfire. He'd had them many times before.

He'd thought maybe trying to get her to relax would help her work out what was causing Gary's problems—maybe they could talk it out together—but instead his plan had completely backfired. When she'd started to sing beautifully with him, he'd lost his head. Watching her in the firelight, the lake behind her shimmering like diamonds, was more than he could take, because it was something he'd always wanted.

That was seven years ago, though.

And he had to keep reminding himself that times had changed—they were just friends—but when she was in his arms, her soft lips against his, his fingers in her silky, soft red hair, it all came rushing back to him.

He was a starving man. He wanted more. So much more and he'd thought for a moment that she wanted the same thing, but when she'd broken off the kiss and pushed him away he realized she didn't and it hurt like hell.

It brought back that moment when he'd woken up to an empty bed and a note that she was leaving for Germany and wishing him the best.

How he'd called out for her, even after he'd read the note because he couldn't quite believe that she'd left him. Even then he'd gotten dressed and driven to her mother's place.

"She's gone," Sandra had said. "She took an early morning flight out to Munich."

"Why didn't she tell me sooner?" he'd asked.

"I told you to let her go before, Reece. She tried to tell you and she almost didn't go. Don't you see this was for the best?"

Only he hadn't seen that because he'd been blinded by love. He'd been so in love with her and her abrupt departure had crushed him.

It was good she'd walked away. It was good it hadn't gone beyond that kiss.

He wouldn't risk his heart again.

As he rounded the corner he caught a glimpse of her, charting at the nurses' station. That silky hair tied back in a braid and wound into a bun so he could see all her creamy white neck as she typed into a tablet.

She was beautiful.

She was like a drug for him and he had to put some distance between them so he didn't forget himself. Last night had been a fluke. His emotions had been running high after singing his father's songs and being found out by someone who knew his father.

Then she'd been there in the alley, waiting for him, and it had been a heady rush escaping off into the woods with her.

It was as if no time had passed between them.

As if she knew someone was watching her, she looked up and their gazes locked across the hall. A slight tinge of pink rose in her creamy-white skin and she smiled at him briefly before turning back to her notes.

And it was obvious in that awkward moment she was feeling the same things as he was. She was regretting the kiss. Just like he was.

Liar.

His pager vibrated and he glanced at it to see that Dr. Brigham was paging him. Reece sighed and turned to make his way to the Chief of Surgery's office at the other side of the hospital.

When he got there he was ushered right in.

"Ah, Dr. Castle, I'm so glad you were able to come see me. Have a seat." Dr. Brigham motioned to the empty chair and sat down behind his desk. Reece sat down. He'd been working with Dr. Brigham long enough to recognize that the man was agitated.

"How can I help you, Chief?"

Dr. Brigham leaned back in his chair and tented his fingers. "I'm sure you've heard the rumors that I'm retiring soon and that I'm looking for another neurosurgeon to take my place. Of course this has ticked off our human resources rep. She thinks that I should pick from a larger pool of surgeons."

"I don't disagree with her," Reece said cautiously.

"I wanted the next chief to take my surgery load. A general surgeon can't do craniotomies."

"No, but you could always pass on your case load to another neurosurgeon and appoint another as chief."

Dr. Brigham frowned. "I don't like it, but I have to do what the Board wants and they agree with the HR representative."

Reece nodded. "So how can I help you?"

"You know the other surgeons well. Could you name some good surgeons in other fields that would be good candidates?"

"Off the top of my head, Dr. Dean, Dr. Anderson and Dr. Morris would fill the position well. They're excellent."

"Thank you."

"Is that all?" Reece asked.

"No, I want your opinion about Dr. Maguire. There have been some concerns raised."

Reece's hackles went up, but he kept his calm. "Oh?"

"She hasn't figured out what's wrong with Mr. Trainer."

"With all due respect, Dr. Brigham, that's a tough case to crack. She's been working hard, running tests and trying to find out what is causing his problems. She's devoting all her time to finding a cure. Has Mr. Trainer complained?"

"No, the patient is absolutely smitten with her. His management team is anxious about it, though. They're threatening to take him to another hospital."

Reece's stomach knotted. "They're losing money and they're worried, aren't they?"

"Yes. They've had to cancel sold-out shows. Mr. Trainer was supposed to go on tour in a couple of days."

He should've known. The management team had no concept of medicine and were geared by the almighty dollar. It didn't matter if a man's life hung in the balance. They were losing money. Gary Trainer was an asset and they wanted him to perform.

Just like his father's manager had forced his father to perform endless hours in that final year. Not caring that a lifetime of substance abuse had taken its toll. They'd worked him until he'd dropped in his grave and he hated to see it happening to Gary. Gary at least didn't take drugs or drink heavily. He just pushed himself too hard. He never stopped working.

"Well, if they force him to perform before we find out what's causing the problem, he'll die. Dr. Maguire and I can't be at every one of his performances holding a defibrillator, waiting for him to collapse."

Dr. Brigham looked taken aback. "I'm sorry, Dr. Castle, but I can't control if they move him to another hospital."

Reece scrubbed his hand over his face. "I understand, but I wouldn't let this taint your judgment of Dr. Maguire. She's a damn fine surgeon."

Dr. Brigham cocked an eyebrow. "I've never heard you speak so passionately for one of your coworkers before or speak so frankly with me. I like it."

"She's a good surgeon. That's all there is to it."

Dr. Brigham sighed. "I brought her here to diagnose a medical mystery and she has yet to do that. Yes, she's a brilliant surgeon, having worked in trauma surgery, but she seems distracted. I expected better of one of Dr. Mannheim's students."

She was your student first. Only Reece bit back that comment. "It's impossible to diagnose a condition that doesn't show up on any tests."

"And what about the distraction aspect? I understand her mother is on your Alzheimer's Trial. I hope that wasn't because you felt like you had to do it for a coworker."

"No," Reece said sharply. "It was purely a medical reason. I had an opening and her mother fit the category. Who wouldn't be distracted by their parent suffering from a condition that has no cure?"

"Exactly my concern."

Reece wanted to utter a few expletives but he decided it was best if he left. "I don't have much more to say, Dr. Brigham. You have my recommendations."

"I do. Thank you, Dr. Castle."

"I have to check on the patients in my trial." He got up and tried to leave.

"I don't understand why you won't recommend yourself, Dr. Castle," Dr. Brigham said. "Any other surgeon who had my ear would convince me that they and *they* alone were the only one to take over my job or my caseload, yet you won't. Do you not want it?"

I do.

Deep down he wanted that recognition, but he didn't think he had what it took to lead a team of surgeons, to lead a hospital on the cutting edge of medical discovery. He didn't have what it took to speak to the press, to deal with management teams, to schmooze and wine and dine the people that had flitted in and out of his parents' life.

"No. No, I don't." And with one last nod of acknowledgment he left Dr. Brigham's office, putting it and Dr. Brigham far behind him. He was angry that Dr. Brigham was being so easily swayed by people who didn't know what they were talking about and he was angry at himself, because even though he'd stepped away from music to get out of his father's shadow he was still on the sidelines. Standing in the shadows.

Invisible and alone.

CHAPTER ELEVEN

"So, how did my replacement do, Doc?" Gary asked her as she reached over and listened to his chest with her stethoscope.

"You're a sneak, you know that."

Gary looked shocked. "Why?"

"You could've told me Dr. Castle was your replacement singer."

"Would you have gone?" Gary asked.

"No," Vivian said. "Probably not."

"Why?" Gary asked. "I can sense there's something going on between the two of you and I have to say I'm a bit jealous."

Vivian rolled her eyes. "There's nothing going on between Dr. Castle and me. We're just colleagues and he's a bit of a private person. He didn't appreciate me showing up."

And she was positive, judging by the way he was avoiding her, that Reece was not happy about what had happened last night at the lake. She'd ended the kiss for both their sakes, but when she'd pushed him away she could see that same hurt and pain he'd had on his face the day she'd walked back into Cumberland Mills.

Vivian kept trying to tell herself that what she'd done was for the best. She couldn't give Reece her heart and she didn't want to hurt him again.

Only she had.

It was clear from the way he was avoiding her and, when their work forced them together, barely even looking at her.

"I think you're lying to me, Doc. There's something there. Were you two involved once? There is something that runs deep there."

"Is there?" Vivian asked, brushing the comment off.

"Oh, yeah. I mean, I do write and sing country music."

Vivian smiled at him indulgently. "Is that a fact? I had no idea."

Gary snorted. "Come on, so what is it? Former lovers, scorned romance? Maybe you guys actually hate each other."

"That's it. I hate Dr. Castle."

Gary snorted again and threw up his hands. "Fine. I give in. I doubt you hate each other. I've watched you two interact. I may have been slipping in and out of consciousness, but I can tell when two people care for each other and you two definitely do."

"So sending me to the Red Swallow Bistro was your way of trying to get us together?"

He nodded. "Yep. I'm a phenomenal matchmaker. Do you know how many couples I've brought together with my songs? My platinum single 'With Every Breath' was the number one wedding song last year."

Vivian sighed. "I hate to disappoint you, but there won't be any wedding in my near future. Dr. Castle and I are just colleagues...friends. That's it."

"Oh, well." Then Gary grinned. "Maybe I'll go after you, then, 'cause you're mighty pleasing on the eyes, Doc."

"Get some rest, Gary. I'm going to be sending you for a CT scan tomorrow."

He frowned. "Another?"

"Sorry. Your body is hiding something from me and I aim to find it."

He leaned back and grinned a devious smile. "I can show you what I'm hiding, Doc. You don't need to send me for a scan."

"Gary, if you don't shut up I'm going to file a harassment report against you," she chuckled. "Get some rest."

"Yes, Doc." Gary then sat up. "Hey, Andrew! What the heck are you doing here?"

Vivian was surprised to see the songwriter from The Red Swallow last night, the one who'd made Reece so uncomfortable, walk into the room.

Andrew recognized her. "Dr. Maguire, isn't it?"

"Yes," Vivian said politely. "Yes, it is."

"You two know each other?" Gary asked.

"Yes," Andrew said. "I met her last night at the Red Swallow. She was sitting with Ray Castille's son—Reece Castle I think he goes by."

Vivian's heart fell as Andrew revealed Reece's greatest secret as if it was no big deal.

"Dr. Castle is Ray Castille's son?" Gary was shocked, his eyes wide. "I can't believe I didn't see it before. It all makes sense now."

Oh, God.

"If you'll excuse me, gentlemen, I have some more rounds to get to."

She had to find Reece and she had to warn him that soon all of Cumberland Mills was going to know that he was Ray Castille's son. For whatever reason, Reece wanted to keep it quiet and she respected that, but not everyone would be so respectful.

She knew how much he hated to be the center of attention.

Vivian left Gary's room and placed his chart back at the nurses' station. "Do you know where Dr. Castle is?"

The nurse looked up and then glanced at her computer.

"He's in OR three. He's doing a protocol for his Alzheimer's trial."

Darn.

She couldn't invade his trial; if she walked in there without permission she could invalidate the whole thing. Approval had to be obtained beforehand and recorded.

"Could you please page down to the OR and ask him to find me before he leaves for the night? Tell him it's important."

"Of course, Dr. Maguire. Where will you be?"

"I'll be in the research lab."

"Not with your mother?"

"No, I saw her earlier. Why?"

The nurse shrugged. "She has another visitor."

"Oh, it's probably a neighbor. Thanks."

Before she headed to the research lab again she decided to check in on her mother after all and see who had come to visit her. Since the protocol had been administered, her mother hadn't had another major blip and Reece was going to release her from the hospital soon as he had administered the trial medications and done all the tests he needed. Vivian had already got a nurse ready to keep her mother company, because she could still have a lapse and until Vivian figured out what was going on with Gary Trainer she would have to spend all her available time at the hospital.

As she approached her mother's room she heard laughter and then a deep chuckle respond to her mother's laugh. It sent a shiver of dread down her spine because she recognized that laugh. It had been a long time since she'd heard it, though.

Please don't be him.

When she walked into the room her world was thrown off kilter by the sight of her estranged father standing by her mother's bedside, holding her hand. An unwelcome apparition from her past. They were laughing and chatting as if no time had gone by. She'd convinced herself that the face she'd seen in the audience that night at the Opry couldn't have been her father. He'd been gone for so long. But she'd been wrong…

"Daddy, don't go!" Vivian had clung to him.

"Come on, Hank, we gotta go!" one of her father's bandmates had whined from the station wagon they were all piled into.

"Vivi, I have to go."

"No, Daddy. No. Please."

He'd pried her off him. "I'll be back."

Vivian had stood there on the sidewalk, watching as her father climbed into that station wagon and drove away. She'd been able to hear her mother sobbing in the kitchen and she'd known he was never coming back. She'd never see her father again.

Yet it was her father. He was standing there, comforting her mother as if he was a good doting husband, but Vivian knew better. She could see through the sheep's clothing to the wolf that lingered below.

He was probably here trying to glean money from her mother. He was probably looking for a handout and Vivian saw red. There had been so many times her mother had worked paycheck to paycheck, earning barely enough to buy food let alone keep a roof over their heads. He'd never been there to help them. He'd never provided for them the way a husband and father was meant to.

"What're you doing here?"

Her father glanced up. "Vivian, it's good to see you again."

She stepped in the room, shutting the door behind her. "I asked what are you doing here?"

"Excuse me, Doctor, but I don't think you should be talking to my husband in such a tone. He has every right to be here. I just had a baby." Her mother's eyes were wild; she was getting riled up.

Vivian's heart sank as she stared into her mother's angry eyes. Her mother was living a moment in the past. The protocol hadn't worked. She'd been holding out so much hope, but now, staring into her mother's eyes, a stranger's eyes, it was apparent the trial wasn't working for her.

"I'm sorry, Mrs. Bowen. I'll leave you alone now, but can I speak to your husband privately?"

Her mother frowned and glared at her before turning back to her father. "Do you mind? Maybe complain to her superior about her rudeness."

"She's just doing her job, Sandra. I'll be right back." He kissed her hand and Vivian repressed the urge to run over there and smack her mother's hand out of his.

Once they were in the hall she motioned to him to follow her to a consult room. Once inside she shut the door.

"Have a seat," she snapped, keeping her hands firmly in her pockets so that she wouldn't be tempted to reach out and throttle him.

"Vivian, I know that my return is a shock."

"So why are you here? If you're looking for a handout you won't get one. I'm her power of attorney."

"I'm not here for money. I'm here to make amends," he said.

Vivian scoffed. "I've heard that one before."

"I mean it this time, Vivi."

"Don't call me that," Vivian snapped. "I'm Dr. Maguire."

"You changed your name?"

"I did."

Her father looked crestfallen. "I guess I deserved that."

"Why are you here?" Vivian asked. "She has Alzheimer's. You do know that, don't you?"

"I do." His voice trembled, but she was used to that.

He was a good actor. "It's why I came back. I came back to take care of her."

"She doesn't need you. You just confuse her. I'm taking care of her, like I've done since I was ten years old."

"I want to make things right, Vivian. Please give me a chance."

Maybe he was sincere, but she'd heard him perform this song and dance before. Like those times once he got what he wanted he'd leave again. Off on another tour, singing in dives and drinking.

Her father wasn't only addicted to liquor. He was addicted to attention and he craved the attention of superstardom that he'd never obtained. Her father was a pathetic excuse for a man. So she didn't answer him when he begged for another chance; instead she opened the door and motioned for him to leave. She was done listening to his sob story.

He sighed. "Look, I'm singing down at the Dead End tonight. Please come see me after my set so I can explain myself. Please. I don't want any money, I don't want handouts."

"I'll think about it, but don't hold your breath."

He nodded, crestfallen. "Okay. I do hope you come, Vivian. I really do."

Vivian stood shaking as she watched him walk down the hallway out of the neuro wing. At least he hadn't gone back to bother her mother.

She took a deep calming breath and tried to fight back the tears of anger that were threatening to spill. When she got a hold of herself she headed back to her mother's room to make sure she was okay.

When she walked in the room, her mother was smiling expectantly, but then her smile disappeared and she glared. "Oh, it's you."

"Mama, it's me, Vivian."

She frowned. "What kind of game do you think you're playing at? You're not Vivian. Vivian is a baby."

"Yes, but Mama that was a long time ago. Don't you remember?" She was trying desperately to shake her out of her setback, to get her mother back.

"No, I don't know what you're talking about. Where's my husband?" Then her mother looked around the room in a panic. "Where is my baby?"

"Mama..."

"Stop calling me that!" Her mother tried to rip the IV from her arm. "I have to get out of here."

Vivian rushed forward and tried to push her back down, but her mother slapped her hard across the face, knocking Vivian back.

"Whoa, Mrs. Bowen. It's okay." Suddenly Reece was there, holding her mother down. "It's okay. I'm Dr. Castle and I'm going to find your husband and baby."

"Get that she devil away from me!" her mother screamed.

Reece glanced over his shoulder. "Get a sedative."

Stunned, Vivian went out into the hallway and accessed the medicine cabinet. She pulled out a mild sedative and a syringe. When she brought it to Reece he had her mother calm. He quickly injected the sedative into her IV line.

"I want my baby and husband, Dr. Castle. They're gone," her mother sobbed, pleading with him. It broke Vivian's heart.

Curse her father for riling her mother up like that. Why did he have to come back?

"I'll find them, Mrs. Bowen. It's okay." Reece's voice was gentle and soothing. "Just rest."

Her mother nodded and slowly fell into a sedated sleep.

"What set your mother off?" he asked.

"My father showed up."

"Your father?"

"Yeah, he's hasn't been around for years. He left us

when I was young. He came back and she just regressed to a happier time."

"What did he want?" Reece asked.

"He wants to make amends. He wants me to meet him tonight at the Dead End."

He frowned. "That's a seedy place."

"That's not surprising for him. He was always known for frequenting those kind of establishments so I guess nothing has changed."

"Is this why you paged me in the OR?" he asked, not looking at her as he checked her mother's vitals.

"No," Vivian said. "That's not it."

"Then what is it?" he asked impatiently.

"Andrew Sampson came to visit Gary Trainer."

The color drained from his face and he frowned. "Did he?"

"Yes. I'm afraid your secret is out."

CHAPTER TWELVE

REECE CURSED UNDER his breath as he stormed out of Vivian's mother's room. He couldn't deal with this now. This was something he never wanted to deal with. As he walked down the hall all eyes turned to him. He could feel the stares, hear the whispers and he knew then there was no kind of damage control he could do. Everyone knew he was Ray Castille's son.

It was washing over this hospital faster than a tidal wave.

Whoever he was before didn't matter. They didn't see him as Dr. Reece Castle anymore. They were looking at him, comparing him to his father, whispering about their estrangement and wondering if he had the same talent as his father and why he didn't choose that life.

It enraged him that they judged him this way. Hadn't he proven himself as a surgeon? He was more than just a country legend's son.

Only that wasn't what anyone saw anymore. They couldn't see beyond his father.

He shook his head and headed for the privacy of his office. He needed time to adjust, to figure out what he was going to do. Then he stopped. No, he was going to face this head-on. He turned and headed to Gary's suite. Now the truth was out, there was no sense trying to deny it any longer.

When he got there Andrew Sampson was sitting by Gary's bedside and chatting with him. The moment Reece walked through the door the conversation stopped.

"Why didn't you tell me, Dr. Castle?" Gary asked. "Your dad was my idol. I can't believe you're Ray Castille's estranged son."

"Yes. I am," Reece said quickly. "And I'm aware that you're fond of my father's music."

"More than fond. He's my inspiration. The stories you must have."

Reece snorted. *Stories. Right.* He had a lot of stories and they mostly consisted of addiction and violence.

Also crushing loneliness.

"No, not any stories. Not really."

"Andrew was telling me how you sang some of your father's songs last night. You have a gift, my friend."

"I know. It's medicine," Reece snapped. He crossed his arms. "I changed my name for a reason. I can't say I'm too impressed that my colleagues now know who my father was."

Andrew frowned. "I'm sorry, Dr. Castille, truly I am. I didn't think that was something you would hide. I mean, he was your father. I thought you would be proud of that."

"I am aware of who he was, Mr. Sampson, and it's Dr. Castle. Not Castille."

"Andrew was telling me that your father's thirtieth anniversary of his first platinum single is coming up. They were asking me if I wanted to sing, but I'm not sure when I'm getting out of here," Gary hedged. "You wouldn't happen to know, would you, Dr. Castle?"

"No, Gary. I don't know. I can hazard a guess that you won't be able to participate in my father's anniversary show at the Opry."

"So how about you?" Andrew asked. "The offer still

stands. It would be a great full circle to have you make your debut at the Opry."

"Debuts at the Opry are for those who are pursuing a singing career, Mr. Sampson. I'm not," Reece said firmly.

"You could be," Andrew said.

"No, I couldn't. I'm not interested." Reece didn't want to stay another moment in the room. He couldn't. He was so angry. All of his years protecting himself from this moment and it was done. He'd known it was a bad idea to sing at the Red Swallow Bistro that night. He didn't know why he'd done it.

Because maybe you secretly wanted everyone to know. You're tired of holding it in.

"Now, if you'll excuse me, gentlemen, I have rounds." He left the room, his pressure still high.

"Reece!"

He turned to see Vivian running after him.

"Not now, Vivian," he snapped and continued to walk away. He tried to shut the door to his office, but she pushed her way in.

"Don't you dare push me aside and run away from me!"

"You ran from me," he growled. Then he groaned, instantly regretting the words. "I'm sorry."

"No, it's okay. I just wanted to check in on you."

"Vivian, I don't have time for this. Go. Please, I'm begging you."

She crossed her arms. "No. I'm not leaving. Why are you so upset about your secret getting out?"

"I don't want the attention."

She sighed. "I'm sorry it happened. I'm sorry for it all."

And he had a sense that she was apologizing for more than just his secret getting out. He sat down wearily in his chair and scrubbed a hand over his face.

"This is not what I needed today. I have three more

protocols to do and I have to send your mom back down to CT."

Vivian nodded. "I think she's regressed."

He nodded. "I think so too and I'm sorry. You said your father was here and that triggered her?"

"I have no doubt." He could hear the bitterness in her voice. Apparently he wasn't the only one with father issues.

"Is your father still here? I mean, you're the power of attorney. You can deny him access to your mother. Especially when she's like this... Plus when you put her into a home."

"I'm not putting her into a home," Vivian said quickly.

"Vivian, be realistic. She's regressing fast. You can't be with her twenty-four seven. You have a life, a career."

"Not much of one, if the rumors are to be believed."

"What rumors?" he asked.

"My skills are being questioned. The board is demanding an answer to Gary's medical condition. An answer I can't give them because I can't find what's causing his problems."

"Don't let them make you doubt yourself, Vivian. You'll find the answer."

She shrugged. "It is what it is. I can only do so much, but with my mother fading perhaps I should just take a sabbatical and take care of her myself."

"And what if she regresses the way she did today? You could get hurt."

"Why do you care?" she asked.

"I just do."

It was killing him not to take her in his arms like he wanted to right now. He was simultaneously angry with her and wanting to protect her. He needed her and he resented her for that.

"I have to take care of my mother. She's all I have."

"You also have a father who wants to make amends."

Vivian rolled her eyes. "So he says."

"I'll go with you if you want." He couldn't believe the words that had just escaped his lips.

"You're going to go with me?"

"Yes. I'll reiterate again that he can't be around my patient. Not while she's in the hospital and a part of my trial."

Relief etched across her face. "Thank you, but you don't have to come with me."

"Of course I do. We're friends, aren't we?"

"Are we?" she asked.

No. He didn't want to be her friend. He wanted to be more. So much more, but that was just impossible.

"Yes. Of course. You were the first person I told about my secret."

"I appreciate it."

"Come on, let's get your mother down to CT while she's sedated and then we'll go down to the Dead End and see if we can find your father."

"And what about your secret?"

"There's no stopping it now. It's out. I'll just have to try and maintain my privacy the best I can." He opened the door and they walked out of his office together.

"Did Andrew ask you to take part in your father's anniversary show again?" she asked.

"He did and I gave him the same answer as I did last night, which was no."

"Are you sure you don't want to do that for your father?"

He frowned. "Do you really want to open up the father can of worms right now?"

"No. Okay, I'll drop it. Let's just get my mother's scans done and see how bad it's regressed."

"If she falls below the five percent margin, she's no longer allowed to be on the trial. I'm sorry."

"I understand. Don't be sorry." Vivian sighed. "And I thought today was going to be an easy day."

Reece chuckled. "Not here. It's never an easy day, it seems."

Vivian couldn't get the conversation with her father out of her head. She still thought meeting him was a mistake, but at least she could reiterate to him that she had the medical power of attorney and that she didn't want him visiting her mother. He'd already done enough damage.

Her mother was in a fragile state.

They wheeled her down to the CT scan and Vivian prayed that her mother hadn't fallen below the margin, so that she could stay in Reece's trial and benefit from the therapies in the other stages of the Alzheimer's trial.

She stood next to Reece, staring at the computer, anxiously waiting for the brain scans to come up.

This was her father's fault.

"Why did he show up?" Vivian muttered. "If he'd only kept away…"

"You can't blame him," Reece said. "Should he have shown up? Probably not, but you can't blame him."

And then she felt guilty for thinking that. How long had she been blaming her father? So long that it was habit.

Reece was right; this wasn't her father's fault. It was the disease that plagued her mother. And right now it was her mother who needed her focus.

Reece grounded her. Made her see all sides. She'd forgotten the effect he had on her. How much she'd missed it.

"Sorry."

He smiled at her. "Don't be sorry. I get it."

She wanted to ask him why he got it, but her mother's scans came up.

"Darn," Reece whispered as he leaned over and looked at the scan. "I'm sorry, Vivian."

Tears threatened to spill, but Vivian wouldn't let them. "It's okay. You said her condition was worsening at an exponential rate. There was nothing you could do. Thank you for giving her a chance in your trial."

He tried to embrace her, but she shrugged him away.

Vivian told herself she didn't need his comfort, even though deep down she knew she did. She wanted it. Craved it, but denied herself it.

"Are you okay?" he asked.

"I'm fine." She took a deep breath. "I have to go finish up a couple things before I head to the Dead End."

"Do you want to go together?"

She did but instead said, "You know what, I think I need to handle it on my own. It'll be better if I just head over there by myself. You have your own problems to deal with."

"If that's what you want."

"It is." And she turned on her heel and left the CT room. If she let Reece come with her, then she would eventually succumb to him again and she couldn't have that. She didn't deserve the happiness it would bring and he didn't deserve the fact that she would end up hurting him again, because she would.

She was too much her father's daughter. She suddenly understood that now. Strong-willed and passionate. Working hard on what she believed in, even if that meant leaving behind the people you loved. And it rocked her to her very core.

I'm just like him.

She swallowed the knot of emotion welling up inside her. How could she be hard on her father when she too had left her mother alone, only visiting a few times in the past seven years because she was too busy with her career? And what good did that do? She couldn't even diagnose Gary Trainer.

But she was here now and this was where she was going to stay.

She wouldn't leave her mother again.

Maybe you need someone else to help you?

It hit her like a ton of bricks. She was looking at the nerves, looking at the organs for a sign of a tumor or some anomaly. She'd looked at the blood and the spinal fluid for something microscopic there, but what if it went deeper into the tissue? Something she couldn't see because it was so small, so hidden that she wasn't even looking for it?

She rushed to her office and pulled up the latest scans from Gary, staring at them like she'd done so many times the past few days. Only this time she saw the faint shadow she'd been missing on the lower left lobe of Gary's lung, hidden behind the liver. The shadow was so faint that his body probably hadn't even started producing enough white blood cells to be noticeable.

And if she was a betting woman she would put all her money on the fact that Gary had a teratoma and was suffering from Lambert-Eaton Myasenthic Syndrome or LEMS. She'd only seen it once before. She hadn't even put it in the realms of thought when she was trying to find what was causing his issues, but now it all made sense. Why he couldn't get oxygen when he sang. Why the pulse oximeter kept dropping. But to prove her theory she needed to get Gary a lung biopsy.

Vivian headed out to the charge nurse. "I need your help, Swain."

Nurse Swain looked up from his scheduling. "What do you need, Dr. Maguire?"

"Who is the best cardiothoracic surgeon here? One that can do a bronchoscopy on a VIP patient ASAP."

"Dr. Spader. I can page him to your patient's room. Who is the patient?"

"Gary Trainer."

Nurse Swain looked surprised. "I thought he was a neuro patient?"

"He is and he still will be if my theory is proven correct."

"Okay, Dr. Maguire. I'll get him down to Mr. Trainer's room."

"Tell him I'll be there waiting for him."

Vivian sent the CT scans to her tablet and then hurried off to meet Dr. Spader outside Gary's room.

"How can I help you, Dr. Maguire?"

"I hear you're one of the best with a bronchoscopy and biopsy of the lungs."

He smiled. "So they tell me."

Vivian brought up the CT scan, zooming in on the area in question. "My patient is suffering from a myriad of strange symptoms. Tests for white blood cells come back a bit above the normal range, but since he's had some fevers that's not uncommon. Spinal taps have come back clear, yet he's had symptoms of seizures, delusion, muscle weakness and rigidity. I suspect LEMS. If we don't do something fast, my patient could slip into a coma and die."

Dr. Spader cocked an eyebrow. "And you think the teratoma is on left lower lobe of the lung?"

"I do."

He studied the CT scan. "It's faint, but there is something there. Whatever it is, it's small and just starting out."

"LEMS symptoms are discovered well before a cancer is, Dr. Spader."

"All right, I'll get my team to prep him for a bronchoscopy first thing in the morning."

"Thank you, Dr. Spader."

"No problem, Dr. Maguire. I hope you're correct. I know you've been struggling with this."

Vivian kept her cool. She knew that rumors were circulating around the hospital about her, she knew that it was jeopardizing the job she was vying for, but right now she didn't care. She just wanted to get Gary better again and on the right track. "Well, if it is what I suspect it is you can understand why I had a hard time finding the source."

"Yes, that is very true."

Vivian thanked Dr. Spader again and headed into Gary's room.

He looked exhausted, his body was tense and clearly in pain. Andrew Sampson had left and she was glad, because the last thing she needed was rumors about her theory circulating outside of the hospital. It was bad enough the press was camped outside, waiting for any news on Gary's condition.

"Hey, Doc. I thought you'd gone home for the night."

"Not yet." She set the tablet down. "Tomorrow you're going for a test."

He sighed. "Another scan?"

"No. You're getting a lung biopsy."

Gary looked confused. "Why?"

"I think you have a growth on your lungs that's causing your neurological symptoms. It's called LEMS."

"LEMS?"

"Yes, but I won't know for sure until we do a biopsy."

"And if it's not that?"

She shook her head. "I don't know, Gary. Unless there's something you haven't disclosed. Though, with the battery of tests you've been through, there's not much about you we don't know except maybe what's causing your seizures."

"I'm not hiding anything, Doc. I have to say I'm tired of the tests, but why not?"

"Get some rest. Dr. Spader will be performing the biopsy tomorrow morning."

"Thanks, Doc."

Vivian left his room. She knew now she had to get ready to see her father, to find out what he wanted so that maybe she could cut him from her life once and for all so she and her mother could finally move on.

CHAPTER THIRTEEN

THE DEAD END was just as bad as it sounded. If not worse. Vivian was wishing she'd allowed Reece to come with her because the moment she stepped into the dive on the wrong side of the tracks she regretted the fact that she was alone.

She kept close to the bar and tried not to draw attention to herself. It didn't take her long to find her father. He was on stage singing one of Ray Castille's songs. Still, after all this time, chasing something that wasn't his. Something that he would never have.

It cut her to the quick and brought back so many unwelcome memories. Of all the times when she was young and spending time in dives just like this, clutching her mother's hand and watching her father through a smoke-filled haze.

As her father finished the chorus, he glanced up and saw her there, giving her that special wink he always used to give her. Vivian looked away, clenching her fists in anger. It took all her strength not to hit him. It made her angry that he thought it could be the same.

As if he didn't know what he'd done.

What he'd destroyed.

And what she hated the most was that she saw the same in herself when she looked at Reece, knowing that she'd destroyed what they could have had when she'd chosen her career over him.

He could've come with you too.

Only Reece hadn't wanted to leave his safety net. He'd told her that time and time again.

Vivian took a seat at the bar and waited for her father.

It didn't take him long to fill the empty bar stool next to her.

"I'm glad you came, Vivian," he said. "I'm glad you're giving me a chance to explain myself."

"I'm not here to listen to your explanation," Vivian said calmly. "I'm here to tell you to keep away from Mom."

Her father looked shocked. "I'm her husband."

Vivian snorted. "You abandoned her. I don't think your claim over her will hold up in a court of law. I'm her power of attorney and a neurosurgeon. A respected physician, not a sleazy lounge lizard."

"It's clear you're angry with me." He scrubbed a hand over his face. "I wish you weren't."

"What do you expect me to be? Happy that you're back? I haven't seen you since I was ten!" Her voice raised and she cleared her throat. "That day you told me you'd be back, but you never came back. You lied to both of us."

"I'm here now," Hank said.

"It's too late."

"Look, I have to complete another set. Please stick around and then I'll be done and we can go somewhere else. Get a coffee and I can explain myself."

"You really don't have anything I want to hear."

"Please. Do this for me. You're wrong about your mother not wanting to see me. You don't know it all." With that, her father left and returned to the stage.

Vivian stood up to leave—no way was she going to stick around to listen to her father rewrite history—but something compelled her to sit back down and then she looked up to see Reece walking into the bar. He was wearing his black cowboy hat, blending in with the crowd.

She didn't know what he was doing here, didn't want him here, but suddenly she was glad he was.

"Reece," she said as he took the seat her father had vacated. "What're you doing here?"

"I think I'm keeping tabs on you." He nodded in the direction of some of the men, who were now shooting him daggers. "I told you this isn't a place for a single girl to go by herself."

"I told you not to come."

He gave her a half smile. "Aren't you glad I didn't listen?"

She grinned. "Very."

"How's it going?" he asked.

"Not well." Vivian sighed. "He wants to explain himself."

"Does it hurt to hear him out?"

"Yes. It does. He left my mother and me." Vivian shook her head. "I really don't know what he could possibly say to me. I know what he wants."

"Do you?" Reece asked.

"Yes, he wants money. He wants a handout. Maybe I should just give him some money and he'll leave again."

"You can't just buy him off," Reece said gently. Then he turned to look at the stage. "He's playing my father's songs."

"That's all he knows. He worshipped your father. He wanted to be like your father, just as famous. He wanted that mansion in Belle Mead. And he was jealous of my mother, who had a shot at a career. So jealous he ruined it for her. That's why she was so adamant about me putting my career first. She didn't want me to make the same mistake she did."

"A mansion in Belle Mead and my father's life is not something to aspire to," Reece said quickly and she could see the pain in his eyes as well.

"Thank you for coming. I know…you didn't have to do this."

"I know, but I wanted to. Your mother is my patient and I wanted to do what was right for her. I want to protect her too. Even if she's not in my trial anymore, she's my patient. I'll take over her file from whichever neurosurgeon was treating her for Alzheimer's."

"Just her general practitioner had seen her. I was planning on finding someone to treat my mother. I thought I had more time."

She didn't tell him that she was regretting the years she'd left her mother behind. That she had realized that she really was no better than her father.

The set ended and she braced herself for dealing with her dad.

He made his way over to them, pausing with uncertainty when he saw Reece.

"I don't believe we've had the pleasure," her dad said, sticking out his hand. "I'm Hank Bowen, Vivian's father."

"Pleasure," Reece said, shaking his hand. "I'm Dr. Castle. I'm treating Mrs. Bowen for her Alzheimer's."

He cocked an eyebrow. "Are you here to tell me to keep away from my wife too?"

"Dad, don't even start," Vivian said. "Dr. Castle isn't here to get involved. He's here to support me and explain Mom's condition to you."

"I know what Alzheimer's is, Vivian." Her father's demeanor had changed so fast, he was sweating and though she didn't smell the liquor she recognized the signs of him drinking.

And if he had been drinking, she didn't want to be around him.

"I think I should go," she said. "You're clearly not in a state to talk about things."

"Don't leave," her father begged. "You need to listen to me, dammit."

Only she couldn't. Tears were beginning to well up in her eyes and she couldn't hide them from Reece. She'd never cried in front of him before and here she was doing just that, in a seedy bar while her father ranted and raved behind her.

"Please get me out of here," she whispered, begging him to save her even though she didn't deserve to be saved by him.

He nodded and put his arm around her, leading her out of the bar.

"Vivian, come back here! I need to explain."

Vivian tried to block his words from her ears as Reece's strong arms came around her and he led her out of the bar. When she was outside, she began to tremble and Reece held her even more tightly. His arms felt so good around her.

She'd missed this and she didn't want to push him away. She needed him. Wanted him. She just wanted him to hold her close all night.

Even if she could only have him for a moment.

"Where's your car?" he asked.

"I took a taxi."

"Come on, I'll take you home." Reece led her over to his truck and helped her in. He slid into the driver's seat and started the engine, pulling away from the Dead End and heading back to the other side of Nashville. "Where do you live?"

Vivian rattled off the address and leaned back against the seat, watching the lights of the street lamps flicker by. He didn't say anything to her and she was appreciative of that. He knew her so well.

She didn't deserve him.

Reece pulled up in front of her house and walked her to the door. She unlocked the door and invited him inside.

"You okay?" he asked.

"No, I'm not. I haven't seen him in so long. I thought I'd gotten over the shock of seeing him at the hospital, but then tonight with him playing in that smoky club…it brought back so many painful memories."

"I understand that. My father wasn't always a super-star."

"I guess you do get it."

"I do." Reece cleared his throat. "I said once long ago we were the same. When you came back I didn't believe it anymore, but now…"

She nodded. "We're the same."

His eyes were sparkling in the dark and she reached up to touch his face, stroking his cheek. He leaned into her touch and reached up to take her hand, moving it away like he'd done countless times before.

"I'm not sure if you should be doing that," he said hus-kily. "If you keep doing that I'm liable to do something I won't be able to stop."

Her pulse quickened with anticipation. "What if I don't want you to stop?"

"Oh, don't say that unless you mean it," he whispered against her neck.

She didn't need to answer him as she took off his cow-boy hat and set it on the side table so she could see all of his face, run her hands through his short hair and stare up into those warm brown eyes she adored.

"Stay with me tonight," she begged. "Just tonight. One more time."

"If I knew better, I'd leave, but thankfully I don't know any better." He cupped her face with his strong hands and kissed her, just like he'd kissed her the other night at his cabin at the lake. She melted into him this time, really melted into him. It had been so long since she'd felt this way. Even though she'd told herself time and time again over their years apart that she was over him. She wasn't and she'd been a fool to try and think that she was.

Reece was the only man for her, but she'd ruined it and she would pay for that mistake the rest of her life. So for tonight she'd enjoy this stolen moment. She grabbed a hold of his flannel shirt and held it tight in her grasp, not wanting to let him go.

Reece's hands left her cheeks to move down her back, teasing her. She arched her body, trying to get closer to him. He broke off the kiss and scooped her up in his arms, carrying her up the stairs toward her bedroom at the end of the hall. They didn't need to say anything as they stood with their foreheads pressed together.

Vivian couldn't remember wanting him this badly before, but in all the years she'd been away she'd thought of him like this. Close to her, his heart racing under her hand. She began to undo the buttons of his shirt, desperate to touch his skin, to run her hands over his chest. She wanted nothing between them.

He slipped out of his shirt and she raked her fingers across his hard, broad, muscular chest, letting her hands trail down to the belt of his jeans, pulling him against her. He grabbed her hands by the wrists, pulling them away to kiss her. Hungrily.

Reece's kisses seared her flesh and she was completely lost to him as his lips trailed down her neck. His hands on her body, undressing her. When she was naked, he brought her to the bed and leaned over her.

She was a fool to deny herself this for so long.

He touched her everywhere, kissing her and making her want him. She arched up against him, her legs wrapped around his waist, clinging to him and begging him to take her. She wanted to forget, tonight. She wanted him to erase everything.

All she wanted was to be in this moment with him.

He moved away and slipped out of his jeans, coming back to the bed, settling between her thighs. They locked gazes as he thrust into her and she shed a tear, emotion overtaking her because though she'd accomplished so much these last seven years, her life was empty and lonely.

She hadn't realized that until this moment, joined with Reece, and it scared her to come to realize in her own way that she loved him and loving him was a dangerous thing indeed and it terrified her.

As she climaxed he kissed her, tenderly wiping the tears from her eyes.

Reece propped himself on his elbow, watching her sleep. City lights were creeping through the slats of her blind, making her creamy-white skin look as if it was glowing. There was a blush to her cheeks and love bites on her neck, which made him smile.

When she'd walked back into Cumberland Mills he'd sworn to himself that this would never happen again but, try as he might, he was lost to her. He couldn't keep away from her. Vivian still owned his heart.

He needed her and that scared him because he just wasn't sure if he could trust her again to not leave and break his heart, but watching her sleep, her delicate hand on her chest, he knew that he would never want another woman as much as he wanted her.

He'd always wanted her.

There had never been another for him.

She had such control over him and it was terrifying because, really, what kind of life could he give her? He didn't know how to be a husband and a father. His only example was his own father and that had been terrible.

"You're nothing, Reece. Country music in your soul and you're throwing it away for what? Nothing. You're nothing."

"I am something, Dad. I am. I'm a healer. When your talent is wasted away, you'll be nothing. I'll always be a doctor."

"Get out of my house!"

"With pleasure."

And those were the last words that he'd ever spoken to his father. He'd walked out of his father's life and pursued his career in medicine. Yet now, looking back, he regretted it.

He wished he could go back and make amends with his father, but it was too late. His father was dead. There was no second chance for them.

Just like there was no second chance for him and Vivian.

Vivian deserved someone who could give her what she wanted. She hadn't had a normal upbringing either, but at least her mother had been there for her. She loved her mother. They had a good relationship. Reece didn't have that with either of his parents. His mother had been a vapid, washed-up country diva who died in a car crash after a night of drinking. He wasn't even sure if his parents had ever truly loved each other and Reece didn't know if he could even give love when he wasn't sure what it was himself. Besides, he still wanted roots and Vivian never had. He couldn't hold on to her. He couldn't be the person to hold her back, no matter how much he wanted her.

There was a buzz and he sighed, realizing that his pager was going off. He got out of bed quietly and made his way to his discarded jeans, pulling out the pager to find he was getting called to the hospital to deal with an emergency.

He sighed with regret. If he left, this spell, this stolen moment with Vivian would end, but he had to go. He pulled on his clothes as quietly as he could, but she stirred.

"Where are you going?" she asked sleepily.

"There's a trauma that's come into the hospital."

"I'll go with you."

"No, you need rest."

She shook her head. "No, it's fine. I want to check on my mother anyways. Let me come. I don't want to be alone."

He nodded. "Okay. Let's go, then."

She dressed quickly and they headed out to his truck. Vivian's house wasn't far from Cumberland Mills and they both changed into their scrubs once they'd arrived. Vivian went off to her mother's room and he headed down to Emergency.

"Dr. Castle, he was demanding you look at him," the trauma doctor on duty said. "It's a stroke. I've started protocol for clot-busting medicine, but he won't take it unless you came here to deal with him."

Reece frowned and pulled back the curtain.

"Well, well. Look who finally showed up." Vivian's father was lying on the bed.

"Mr. Bowen, you need to take the medicine Dr. Hayden prescribed. You're having a stroke and this will help reverse the damage."

Hank just shook his head. "I haven't touched liquor in years. She wouldn't listen, you know. She wouldn't hear me out when I tried to tell her that her mother and I made amends two years ago. I'm clean." He tried to dig in his pocket and pulled out an AA chip, holding it up.

"Mr. Bowen, please take the medicine or I will have to restrain you."

Hank threw the chip at him, but it didn't get far as his left arm dropped like a sack of bricks and his eyes rolled into the back of his head. The monitor flatlined.

Reece cursed under his breath and pushed the alarm. "I need a crash cart in here stat!" He began CPR as Dr. Hayden lowered the bed flat.

He wasn't going to let Mr. Bowen die before Vivian had

a chance to make amends with her father. He wouldn't let her suffer the way he did every day. He couldn't let her live with the guilt of unfinished business with her father.

Vivian leaned over and kissed her mother on the cheek. Her mother opened her eyes and smiled. Vivian breathed an inward sigh of relief that her mother recognized her. She wasn't sure her heart could take her mother calling her names and trying to assault her again.

"Vivian, what're you doing here?"

She shrugged. "One of my patients has a surgery in a couple hours. A surgery I'm waiting results on. I couldn't sleep so I thought I'd come see you."

"That's nice." She closed her eyes. "Why was I sedated? The nurses said I was sedated when I woke up in the recovery room."

"You had a very bad blip, Mama. I'm glad you don't remember." And she was. She didn't want her mother to remember that her father had been in this room and that her mother had slapped her. It would hurt her mother to know that she'd done that.

"Oh, has it gotten worse?" Sandra asked.

Vivian nodded. "I'm so sorry, Mama. You're no longer a candidate for the Alzheimer's trial. As soon as Dr. Castle discharges you, you'll have to go home."

Her mother frowned. "I'm sorry."

"There's nothing to apologize for. It's not your fault you have this disease."

Sandra nodded. "So what will we do? Your job? You were looking for that promotion."

Vivian shook her head. "Not anymore. I resigned from consideration. I'll just drop down to part-time hours and focus on my research."

"No, you can't do that. Your career is important to you." Sandra tried to sit up. "You gave up so much to obtain the career you deserved. The career you wanted. I'm so proud that you were able to follow your dreams when I couldn't. Your job is too important and you can't cut back."

"You are important too, Mama. More important than any job." She sighed. "When I'm at the hospital we'll get a nurse in to help you."

"I don't need a nurse, Vivian."

"You do, Mama. You…" She trailed off, but couldn't hold it in anymore. "Dad was here."

Her mother didn't seem surprised by this. "Oh, he came back."

"You don't seem shocked by this. Mama, he hasn't been around since I was ten."

Sandra sighed. "No, he's been around the last two years. He's sober."

"What?"

"He's sober. I know his sponsor at AA. It took a lot of rebuilding, but he was the man I fell in love with once again."

"He's just looking for a handout."

"No, darlin', he's not. I was going to tell you that night you came home. The night I had the blip."

"Then where was he those first few weeks I was back in Nashville?"

"On tour. He's still a musician, he still goes on tour. I was crushed when I got this diagnosis and I couldn't go out on tour with him anymore."

Vivian shook her head in disbelief. "How can you fall for this?"

"Fall for what? We've made our peace, Vivian." Then her mother glared at her. "What did you do?"

"He wanted to talk to me and I didn't want to hear it."

"Vivian!"

She shook her head. "No. I don't believe he's changed.

I saw him tonight. He was sweaty and slurring. He was using again."

Her mother's lips quivered. "I don't believe you."

"Trust me. That's why I told him to stay away from you and as your power of attorney I'm going to make sure that happens." Vivian didn't want to discuss it further. Her mother was always easily duped by her father.

As she walked out into the hallway she bumped into Dr. Brigham.

"Dr. Brigham, I'm surprised to see you here in the middle of the night."

"Yes, well, we had a long board meeting. I got your email withdrawing from consideration, and I wanted to ask what made you change your mind. I heard that you may have cracked Gary Trainer's case."

"I have some personal family reasons to withdraw. As you know, my mother has Alzheimer's." And it hit Vivian suddenly that she wasn't a machine, that she had a purpose in life bigger than growing her career. When she'd first arrived she would have never considered withdrawing but, being with her mother again and realizing how important she was and how she'd neglected her, she'd come to see she didn't want the position any longer.

"I respect that, Dr. Maguire. Keep me posted on Mr. Trainer's condition."

"Can I make a suggestion, Dr. Brigham?"

"Of course, Dr. Maguire." He crossed his arms.

"I think the next chief should be Dr. Castle. I know he hasn't thrown his hat in the ring, but he's an excellent surgeon and a good diplomat. He cares about his patients. I think he'd be the right fit for the surgical program at Cumberland Mills."

Dr. Brigham nodded. "Thank you, Dr. Maguire. I appreciate your thoughts."

Vivian nodded and headed off to the on-call room to

catch a nap before Gary's bronchoscopy. She planned to be standing in that lab, watching them as they analyzed the biopsy. She wanted to be there the moment they found the teratoma and confirmed her suspicions that it was Lambert-Eaton Myasthenic Syndrome.

As she headed to the on-call room on the neurology floor Reece rounded the corner, his expression serious.

"Vivian, can you come with me?" He didn't give her much of a choice as he took her arm and led her to an ICU room.

"What's wrong—do you need a consult?"

He shook his head. "I need your permission to do a surgery on a stroke patient."

"Why do you need...?" She trailed off as she looked into the ICU room and saw her father hooked up to machines.

A knot formed in her stomach as she stared at him there. "How did it happen?"

"He came in belligerent and demanding to see me."

Vivian nodded. "Well, do what you have to do."

"Is that all you have to say?" Reece asked, confused.

"What do you want me to say? Alcohol or drugs sent him in here with a stroke."

"Vivian, he's sober. We did a blood alcohol test to be sure. It's zero and his tox screen came back negative."

She shook her head. "I don't believe it. I just can't."

"It would explain his irrational behavior from earlier tonight."

It would, but she didn't know what to think about it. Didn't know if she could believe that her father had really changed.

"Fine—do the surgery." She tried to leave but Reece stopped her.

"Why are you so angry at him?"

"Why are you so angry at your father?" Vivian snapped.

"It's not just him. I'm mad at myself. He wanted to make

amends and I ignored him, just like you're doing right now, and I'm angry that he never loved me enough. Your father loves you, Vivian. I can see it."

She shook her head. "It's not the same thing. Your father was at least there. My father wasn't. And you're one to talk about making amends. You refuse to honor your father at the Opry for his anniversary. Now who's the one holding grudges? You have no right to judge me."

His eyes were like thunder. "You think my father was there? He wasn't. He was too busy partying. I spent two years of my life without sunlight because my father insisted on partying the night away and sleeping all day. But even in spite of that I still hate myself for ignoring him when he reached out to me. Don't blow it, Vivian. Don't walk away from him. You have two parents who love you."

"Wrong, I have one parent who loves me. That's it. My father made it clear that I don't deserve his love."

"You deserve love."

She shook her head. "No, because I have no love to give. I have nothing."

"And don't I know it," Reece snapped.

"What do you mean by that?"

"You're selfish."

It took Vivian back at first, but what did she honestly expect? This storm between them had been brewing for some time.

"I always told you up front what I wanted from my career," Vivian said.

"Munich, though? That was a bit of a surprise."

"I told you that I wanted to work with Dr. Mannheim and you knew that his clinic was in Munich. I wanted to be a diagnostician. That's what I've always wanted. I was always up front with you."

"Then if you didn't want a relationship why did you have to kiss me that day after the solo surgery?"

"I thought you just wanted a fling too."

"Six months together is hardly a fling, Vivian. I wanted more."

"I know," she said. "You wanted roots in Nashville and I didn't. That's why I didn't ask you to come with me."

"You never even gave me the choice to say yes or no."

"Would you have said yes to Germany?" she asked. "Tell me the truth."

"No. Probably not."

She smirked. "See, we wanted different things. And that's why I left."

"I wanted you!" Reece shouted.

"But…you knew I didn't want that. My career, that's all I wanted."

"I didn't care. I loved you. I was irrational. Those roots I wanted were with you."

"Oh, Reece."

"Don't. I don't need your sympathy now," he raged. "You crushed me when you left. Destroyed what little trust I had."

"I couldn't give you what you wanted. I don't believe that kind of love exists and I didn't think you did either."

"I didn't, but I *wanted* to believe in it. I didn't have it when I was a child and you had it all." He shook his head. "That kind of love does exist and I feel sorry for you. What a lonely life you must lead. How unhappy you've been."

The barb hit close to home because she *had* been lonely. She'd loved her job but she'd been alone over there and there were many times she'd questioned her decision to leave. She'd always reminded herself that there was too much hurt in Nashville, but there was part of her that had always wondered what could've been.

No one had ever gotten her like Reece had. They were the same. They belonged together, but that was all ruined now. She'd destroyed any chance. A tear slipped down her cheek. "I'm sorry I crushed your heart."

She turned on her heel and left. She needed to be by herself. Alone, because wasn't that what she'd always wanted anyway?

No. But it was too late for her to come to that realization.

CHAPTER FOURTEEN

VIVIAN WATCHED THE clock as she stood outside the lab waiting for the biopsy on Gary's lung, but she wasn't watching the clock because she was waiting for the results. She was watching the clock knowing that Reece was in surgery trying to save her father's life.

She tried to tell herself that she didn't care, but she did.

It was killing her wondering what was happening and whether her father would live or die. It would crush her mother to lose him. And though Vivian couldn't understand why her mother still loved her husband after all this time it made her wonder if maybe, just maybe, love did exist.

Reece was right. She never gave her father the benefit of the doubt. It was just easier to push it all away. Vivian had felt her father's abandonment so keenly but had always felt a need to be strong for her mother.

She had never truly realized that her father was the first man to break her heart and it was because of him that she pushed everyone away and believed that she didn't deserve love or happiness.

If her father died before she had a chance to listen to him, to make amends and forgive him it was going to eat away at her. Just like Reece had said.

"Dr. Maguire, I have the result for you." The lab tech

held out the sheet and Vivian grabbed it quickly, thanking him as she scanned the sheet.

And there it was.

It was a teratoma on the left lobe of the lung. It had just started to rear its ugly head and when blood was drawn just before the surgery the white blood count had finally elevated enough to raise a flag.

She was right. It was Lambert-Eaton Myasthenic Syndrome. That was causing all of Gary's symptoms. Dr. Spader had told her the sample he took the biopsy from was so small that he'd resected the entire spot. Gary would need chemo but, without his body attacking the teratoma, he would regain function again, although slowly.

Vivian arranged an oncology consult for Gary and then went to meet with Gary's managers with Dr. Brigham.

"Well?" Dr. Brigham asked.

"It's LEMS," Vivian announced.

Dr. Brigham grinned. "You're sure?"

"Positive." She handed the lab result to him.

"What is LEMS?" Gary's manager Buzz asked, scratching his head.

"Gary had a teratoma, a cancerous growth starting on his lung. The problem was we couldn't see it, but his body could. LEMS is a paraneoplastic syndrome," Vivian said.

"In English, please," Buzz groaned.

"His body was not only attacking the growth, but it was attacking him. Every other test came back clean before because it was so minor that it wasn't showing. It's almost like a stage zero. The growth was disrupting his neuromuscular transmission. That's why he was having seizures among other things," she said.

"So will he need to have chemo?" Buzz asked.

"I've asked for an oncology consult," Vivian said. "He

will need some chemo, but not for long. The surgeon who did the biopsy was able to resect the entire growth."

"Excellent work, Dr. Maguire."

Vivian nodded in deference to Dr. Brigham. She was relieved that she'd finally solved the mystery. She'd encountered LEMS only once before and that was a long time ago. It was something unexpected.

Just like falling for Reece again. No. Not again. She'd never fallen out of love with him.

She shook that thought away and left Gary's room. It was then that she saw Reece wheeling her father's gurney into an ICU room. Reece didn't look at her. He hadn't looked at her since their blowup earlier.

She regretted the words she'd said to him.

She regretted a lot of things. Most of all hurting Reece, because he was right; she was unhappy. Lonely. And she'd come to the painful realization that career wasn't everything. Love was. Only it was too late.

As if he knew she was looking at him, he looked back, but his expression was just as cold as the day she'd walked back into Cumberland Mills.

She wanted to find out how her father was, but she couldn't bring herself to go over and talk to Reece.

You don't deserve him.

She wanted to just turn and walk away, but she couldn't. Before she knew what she was doing she was walking over to the ICU room and standing in the doorway.

"Can I help you?" Reece asked without glancing back at her.

"How is he?"

"He lived, but it was bad. I won't lie to you. He may have brain damage. He wouldn't take the clot-busting medicine when he first came in. He was so adamant to prove to me that he'd changed." Reece reached into his pocket and pulled out an AA chip and placed it in her hand. "He brought this in. Two years sober."

Reece left her then, standing in the ICU by her father's bed.

Vivian stared at the chip in her hand. Her father had been telling the truth. Her mother too. Maybe he had changed. All this time she hadn't thought people could change, but maybe they could.

You've changed so why not him?

She had changed on the outside maybe, but inside she still carried pain and she didn't know why she hadn't dumped the extra baggage a long time ago. She squeezed the AA chip in her hand. She *had* changed, just in a way she'd never thought was possible and she was glad for the change she wasn't expecting.

It was then that she wept, standing by her father's bedside. He'd begged her to listen, but she'd been so mad. Maybe if she had she would've seen the signs of stroke earlier, but she'd been just as stubborn and pigheaded as he was. Everyone deserved a second chance.

"Oh, Dad." She reached out and squeezed his hand. "I'm so sorry. I forgive you. Don't go."

The hand squeezed back and she smiled as his eyes opened briefly, but just briefly.

"I'm sorry, Dad. I'm so sorry." She held up the chip. "Thank you."

There was a faint smile and a slight nod as if he understood her. It was a faint glimmer of hope and she breathed a sigh of relief. He didn't let go of her hand though, so she pulled a chair over.

"Okay. I'll stay. I'm right here."

"Dr. Castle, can I speak with you a moment?"

Reece stopped to see Dr. Brigham motioning for him

to join him in the conference room. Reece groaned. He didn't have time for this.

"How can I help you, Dr. Brigham?" He froze in his tracks when he realized that it wasn't just Dr. Brigham in the room, but the board of directors. "How can I help all of you?"

"We've made our decision about who will become the next Chief of Surgery."

Reece nodded. "Okay. That's fantastic. Is it Dr. Maguire?"

"No, Dr. Maguire withdrew from consideration yesterday," Brigham said as if it was common knowledge and not really that important.

"What?" Reece asked in disbelief. He couldn't believe that she'd walked away from the job. When she'd returned to Cumberland Mills she'd made it clear she was after Dr. Brigham's job as Chief of Surgery.

"I have aspirations on Dr. Brigham's job. Who wouldn't?"

Her words came back to haunt him.

"Did she say why?"

"No, and it doesn't matter as she actually recommended you."

"Me? I'm not interested, Dr. Brigham. You know my reasons."

"And they're moot at this point. The board agrees you should take over as Chief of Surgery. We understand you'll want to continue your Alzheimer's trial so I will be offering my practice to Dr. Maguire, who has agreed to carry on as a part-time surgeon."

Reece was taken aback. "She's part-time?"

"Yes. She's asked for a cutback in hours for personal reasons. And that's fine. My question now is—do you accept?"

He didn't know how to answer that. He'd always flown under the radar and stood in the shadows.

"Well, Dr. Castle? Do you accept?"

Reece nodded. "Thank you."

Dr. Brigham nodded. "I've always thought you were right for the job, Reece. Always. I just wish you hadn't made me go on such an extensive search before deciding that you actually deserved this job."

"I'm sorry about that, sir. It won't happen again."

"See that it doesn't."

Reece chuckled and left the boardroom in shock and then dismay to learn that Vivian had stepped away from the position and that she was dropping her hours. She was such a talented surgeon. It was such a waste.

Can you blame her?

He'd given her such a hard time about her father when he couldn't even deal with his own issues about his dad. There was guilt for not seeing him on his deathbed and that was why he couldn't go out on that stage at the Grand Ole Opry and sing his songs.

It wouldn't be right when he was such a terrible son all those years ago, letting bitterness and hate eat away at him. It had gotten him nowhere. That was why he'd snapped at Vivian. He didn't want her to go through the same thing as him.

But she had been right. He was never going to be able to bury the ghost of his father or all the hurt and move on with his life if he didn't get up on that stage and sing his father's songs, like his dad had always wanted him to do.

When he walked past the ICU he was shocked to see that Vivian was still sitting by her father's bedside, her hand in his.

Maybe she'd forgiven, but could he?

"You withdrew from consideration," he whispered as he stood in the doorway.

She shrugged. "It was for the best. I didn't deserve that position. You did. You stayed here and worked hard. You think you're always standing in a shadow and are never good enough to step in that spotlight, but you are."

Reece didn't know how to take her compliment. "How is he?"

"He squeezed my hand and seemed to recognize me. Thank you. You were right."

"About what?"

"I would've regretted not forgiving him. Thank you."

Reece nodded quickly and left the room because she'd found that peace and forgiveness but he wasn't sure if he had yet. He wasn't sure if he could ever let go of the past and step out of his father's shadow.

He wasn't sure if he was strong enough, and if he couldn't face that fear, then how could he ever expect to deserve Vivian's love? The answer was simple.

He would never know unless he tried.

CHAPTER FIFTEEN

Three weeks later

THE DOORBELL RANG INCESSANTLY.

Great. Every time she was at the other end of the house someone always came to the door. She'd managed to get a nurse in to help with her parents, but she'd taken time off to make sure they were settled. Her father was expected to make a full recovery from his stroke, though he was still having grip issues that he needed to work on, so he wouldn't be doing any tours or singing on stage any time soon.

But he seemed fine with that, saying that his last tour was just that. His last. He'd come home to take care of Sandra and once he was back on his feet he planned to do so.

Vivian's mother had her good and bad days still, but the nurse was helping with that and, surprisingly, she noticed that her mother was less likely to have a lapse when her father was around.

She was nervous about going back to work and working under Reece. She'd heard through the grapevine that since Dr. Brigham stepped down Reece had implemented a lot of changes and streamlined how things worked at the hospital.

Vivian was thrilled for him. She'd always known that he had it in him. Though he'd always shunned positions like this, but he was a natural born leader. He just didn't see himself like that.

The doorbell rang again.

"I'm coming!" Vivian shouted as she ran down the stairs. The nurse was heading for the door, but Vivian waved her off with a smile and opened the door to a courier.

"Dr. Maguire?"

"Yes."

He handed her an envelope. "Can you sign here?"

Vivian signed the tablet. "There you go."

"Great, thanks! Have a good day."

Vivian shut the door and stared at the small envelope.

"What is it, Vivian?" her father asked from the living room.

"An envelope for me." Vivian wandered into the living room and sat down in her favorite comfy chair.

Her father turned away from the TV to watch her open the envelope.

"What is it?" he asked again.

"It's a note from a patient I treated—Gary Trainer, actually—and he's enclosed a backstage ticket to the Grand Ole Opry tonight."

Her father smiled. "Is that so? Well, you have to go. Tonight is a special night."

"Why do you say that?"

"It's Ray Castille's anniversary show. They're performing at the Ryman tonight and they're going to broadcast it on television. You have to go, Vivian. For my sake."

"Okay, Dad, I'll go. Don't get overexcited."

He frowned. "I'm not. I just think you need to go."

"Gary said he's making his debut return, but he won't be singing. Just doing some introductions tonight. I'm not sure if his vocal cords are ready yet. They're still healing from all his intubations and his lung capacity is not the same anymore."

Vivian smiled as she thought about Gary. Thankfully, he hadn't needed chemotherapy after all. The biopsy had perfectly removed the teratoma and the LEMS symptoms soon disappeared after that. Which was good if he was planning on being on stage tonight.

"He's going to send a car around in…two hours!"

Her father chuckled. "Then you better get ready. The nurse is staying tonight because you were going to the hospital to do some research, so now you can go to the Opry and take pictures."

Vivian rolled her eyes. "I wouldn't know what to take pictures of, Dad."

He laughed. "Go get ready. We'll be fine."

"Okay." Vivian headed upstairs to her room to find something to wear. Or at least find the outfit she'd worn the first time she went to the Opry, when she'd been standing backstage with Gary and Reece.

She had been hoping to see him tonight when she went to do her research. Though she didn't know what to say to him. He clearly wasn't interested in a relationship. He'd made it clear that night he came to check on her and her dad in the ICU. He'd admitted that he had nothing to give anyone.

So she'd given up hope that he'd ever change. And that was fine. She'd had a few stolen moments with him and that made it all worth it. She would gladly work under him at the hospital. She still stood by her belief that he was an excellent surgeon. That hadn't changed.

She got ready and by the time she was coming down the stairs she could see a limo waiting for her outside.

"Are you sure you're going to be okay, Dad?"

"I'm fine," he said. "You look beautiful."

"I checked on Mom and she's sleeping. Betty is in the kitchen."

"Would you go already?" He stood up and gave her a quick kiss on the cheek. "One of us has to make it to the Opry."

"I won't be late."

"You will," her father called as she shut the door.

Gary got out of the limo as she approached. He looked a bit thinner, but overall it was good to see him healthy and smiling.

"Doc, you're a sight for sore eyes." He gave her a quick peck on the cheek. "Thanks for coming with me. You were with me last time and I wanted to make sure you're there this time. Just in case."

"Gary, you were given a clean bill of health. You don't need me there."

He held open the door for her. "I'm a superstitious guy. Just humor me."

She slid into the limo and he followed her in. They chatted about trivial stuff as they made their way to the Opry. His limo pulled up and she couldn't believe the crowds of fans that were waiting.

"Sorry, this is a mandatory part. You're arm candy tonight, Doc." He opened the door to screaming fans and then helped her out, ushering her through the crowd as quickly as he could.

They made their way backstage and had a drink in the green room. When the show started he led her to the side stage.

"Time for me to announce our special guest." Gary headed out on stage and Vivian watched, enjoying herself.

"Thank you all for being here. It's my privilege and honor to be standing up here tonight to honor one of my idols, Ray Castille. Thirty years ago today he was inducted into the Grand Ole Opry and his first single went platinum. They say the good always die young and Ray was no exception. So please give a big warm welcome to his son, Reece Castille, who will be singing his number one hit 'My Heart is Yours.'"

Vivian was shocked as Reece entered from stage left and stood in that spotlight in front of the Grand Ole Opry with his guitar. Smiling and waving to the sold-out show at the Ryman and to all those who were watching on television.

"Thank you all for having me here tonight. It's my pleasure to sing for my father tonight and honor his last wish." Then he turned and faced her, not the audience, as he began to pick at his guitar. As if he'd known that she was there all along, standing in the shadows watching him singing in disbelief, the words of his father's song spilling out as he sang to her.

Vivian could feel the tears in her eyes and, just like that night at the Red Swallow Bistro, he captured her with his music, the song bringing back welcome memories instead of painful ones. Her heart felt as if it was going to burst and he moved toward her, the spotlight following him.

Gary was behind her then, pushing her forward. "Go on, Doc. The song is for you."

She began to shake as she headed out onto stage, joining him as he began to sing the chorus she knew so well and prompting her to join him. To sing the words of her heart. Words that she'd never thought she would ever be able to share with him.

When the song ended, the audience cheered and Reece set down his guitar and moved toward her, holding out his hand.

"What're you doing?" she whispered.

"I think I'm asking you to join me on stage." There was a twinkle in his eyes.

"Why? I don't deserve this. I hurt you."

"The only hurt I suffered was when we were apart. When you weren't with me. That's what hurt the most. I missed you, Vivian. I love you."

"Are you sure?" she whispered.

"I think so," he teased.

"You think?" she teased. "I think you should be certain."

"I know and I am. My life is not complete without you. You think you don't deserve love, but you do. I love you. Only you."

Tears began to stream down her face and she could barely get the words out. "I love you too."

She hadn't been sure about love in the beginning, but she was sure about it now. She needed Reece. Her life wasn't complete without him.

"So will you come out here with me?" he asked again.

She nodded and took his outstretched hand, letting him guide her on stage.

"I love you so much. I should've never left. I should've never let you go," she whispered against his neck. "I'm sorry for leaving you so long ago. I was a fool."

"No. Not a fool. We just weren't ready for our moment in the spotlight."

Vivian laughed and he kissed her. She could hear the audience cheering as he kissed her on stage.

"Does that mean you're giving up medicine to take your father's place?" she teased when the kiss ended.

There was a scream from the audience and Vivian forgot that this moment was a very public spectacle on the Ryman stage, worthy of any country superstar, and now she'd inadvertently hinted that he would be taking up his father's torch.

He covered up his microphone. "Thanks for that."

"Sorry," she whispered.

The crowd was chanting for Reece and he waved to

them. "Maybe I'll do the odd show here and there. Just for him. And, just for him, can you sing another song with me?"

Vivian nodded. "What should we sing?"

Gary walked out onto stage. "How about we sing one of mine?" He slung his arms around Reece and Vivian.

"You shouldn't be singing. You haven't been cleared yet."

"I cleared him today," Reece whispered in her ear. "He's fine."

Gary nodded. "And I feel like singing again. Give it up for the surgeons who saved my life!"

The crowd cheered and Vivian buried her head into Reece's shoulder, then she whispered in his ear, "I don't know any of his songs. Remember I don't like country music!"

The band started up and Gary took center stage, motioning for them to join him.

"You'll have time to learn."

Vivian laughed and took her spot beside Reece, his arm around her while he sang with Gary. She had no doubt she'd learn some new music and maybe even warm up to it.

EPILOGUE

One year later

VIVIAN FOUND REECE sitting down by the lake at their cabin. They'd gotten married a month ago and had spent that month relaxing by the lake. Her father had recovered fully from his stroke and with the help of a full-time nurse he was able to take care of her mother.

So, with her dad stable and a nurse in residence, it was enough reassurance to allow Vivian to move out of her parents' home and into Reece's. She wasn't sure about the commute to the hospital, especially now, but she hadn't told him that. She brought him a cup of coffee in one hand and a glass of orange juice for her.

He was down by the lake with his guitar, writing music. He didn't plan on performing it, but Gary had got Reece into writing songs for him and Reece found it was a great way to relieve stress and come to terms with his own hurt. A way to honor his father and say goodbye. A way for him to lay the ghost of Ray Castille to rest.

He had a real talent for it according to Andrew Sampson, who was now working as Reece's publisher. Still Reece's passion was for Cumberland Mills. As well as her. Vivian didn't doubt that.

"Here you go," Vivian said, setting the coffee cup down on the table next to the wooden bench. "How's it coming?"

"Almost done," Reece said. "I'm sad our honeymoon is almost over. It's been a great month."

Vivian smiled. "It has, but I'm looking forward to heading back to the OR tomorrow."

"What are you doing in the OR tomorrow?"

"Another glioma. Not on the brain stem. Don't look so excited. Dr. Berlin is coming to assist."

"She's really taken a shine to neurosurgery since you called her down from the observation room that day."

Vivian nodded. "I saw so much of myself in her. I wanted to give her a chance, but I didn't want her to be pressured and set up for failure like my first surgeries had been done."

"Only you didn't fail," Reece said.

"And I have you to thank for that." She sighed. "So it's a busy day in the OR tomorrow. I'm looking forward to it."

He chuckled. "Sounds better than my day tomorrow."

"I thought you were starting phase two of your trial. That's exciting."

"True, starting phase two is exciting. The board meeting is not."

"Well, you're the Chief of Surgery," she teased.

"Which is exactly why I didn't want it. In fact you're the one I should blame for that position. You're the one who suggested me, after all."

"Yes, I did and come on, admit it, you did want that position. It was your job. It always was. You love that hospital and you're the best person for the job." She leaned over and kissed him.

Reece grumbled and took a sip of his coffee. "Thanks, this is great."

Vivian sighed. "I know. I'm going to miss coming out here every morning and watching you write, though. It's been so peaceful. I can't remember ever being this relaxed before."

Reece grinned and then waggled his eyebrows. "It's all the exercise you're getting."

She laughed. "Yes, that too."

Reece set his guitar down and then wrapped his arms around her. "Maybe tomorrow you can slip away from your busy day and we can find an on-call room again."

"And what kind of example would you be setting for your residents?"

He shrugged. "I don't care. All I care about at this moment is getting you back into bed."

"No way. I'm not going back to bed. I'm feeling a bit nauseous this morning. Drink your coffee and get that song for Gary done before he comes banging on our door."

"Fine." Reece picked up his guitar and then he eyed the orange juice she was holding. "You're not having coffee? You always have coffee."

"Nope. Orange juice is better for me. Folic acid. It helps prevent spina bifida, among other things." She smiled secretly to herself as she took a sip of her orange juice. He was so involved with his songwriting he didn't get the hint.

Reece snorted. "Now, why are you worrying about folic acid and spina bifida…? Vivian!" He shouted that last bit as he set down his guitar. "Are you telling me what I think you're telling me?"

"Yes, I'm afraid I am, Doctor. And, since you're Chief of Surgery, I'm going to have to ask you for some maternity leave."

Reece shouted again and pulled her into his lap, kissing her.

"I take it you're happy, then?" she asked.

"I am." He took the glass of orange juice and set it down. "So happy, in fact, I'm going to show you just how happy I am."

Vivian laughed as he picked her up and swung her

around, kissing her. A kiss that started off innocently enough but then deepened into something more.

"Be careful, Doctor, or I'm going to want a bit more."

He chuckled. "How much more?"

She slung her arms around his neck. "Your whole heart."

"You already have that. You have it all." And he kissed her again, as if he was never going to let her go.

* * * * *

If you enjoyed this story, check out these other great reads from Amy Ruttan

PERFECT RIVALS...
HIS SHOCK VALENTINE'S PROPOSAL
CRAVING HER EX-ARMY DOC
ONE NIGHT IN NEW YORK

All available now!

MILLS & BOON®
Hardback – August 2016

ROMANCE

The Di Sione Secret Baby	Maya Blake
Carides's Forgotten Wife	Maisey Yates
The Playboy's Ruthless Pursuit	Miranda Lee
His Mistress for a Week	Melanie Milburne
Crowned for the Prince's Heir	Sharon Kendrick
In the Sheikh's Service	Susan Stephens
Marrying Her Royal Enemy	Jennifer Hayward
Claiming His Wedding Night	Louise Fuller
An Unlikely Bride for the Billionaire	Michelle Douglas
Falling for the Secret Millionaire	Kate Hardy
The Forbidden Prince	Alison Roberts
The Best Man's Guarded Heart	Katrina Cudmore
Seduced by the Sheikh Surgeon	Carol Marinelli
Challenging the Doctor Sheikh	Amalie Berlin
The Doctor She Always Dreamed Of	Wendy S. Marcus
The Nurse's Newborn Gift	Wendy S. Marcus
Tempting Nashville's Celebrity Doc	Amy Ruttan
Dr White's Baby Wish	Sue MacKay
For Baby's Sake	Janice Maynard
An Heir for the Billionaire	Kat Cantrell

MILLS & BOON®
Large Print – August 2016

ROMANCE

The Sicilian's Stolen Son	Lynne Graham
Seduced into Her Boss's Service	Cathy Williams
The Billionaire's Defiant Acquisition	Sharon Kendrick
One Night to Wedding Vows	Kim Lawrence
Engaged to Her Ravensdale Enemy	Melanie Milburne
A Diamond Deal with the Greek	Maya Blake
Inherited by Ferranti	Kate Hewitt
The Billionaire's Baby Swap	Rebecca Winters
The Wedding Planner's Big Day	Cara Colter
Holiday with the Best Man	Kate Hardy
Tempted by Her Tycoon Boss	Jennie Adams

HISTORICAL

The Widow and the Sheikh	Marguerite Kaye
Return of the Runaway	Sarah Mallory
Saved by Scandal's Heir	Janice Preston
Forbidden Nights with the Viscount	Julia Justiss
Bound by One Scandalous Night	Diane Gaston

MEDICAL

His Shock Valentine's Proposal	Amy Ruttan
Craving Her Ex-Army Doc	Amy Ruttan
The Man She Could Never Forget	Meredith Webber
The Nurse Who Stole His Heart	Alison Roberts
Her Holiday Miracle	Joanna Neil
Discovering Dr Riley	Annie Claydon

MILLS & BOON®
Hardback – September 2016

ROMANCE

MILLS & BOON®
Large Print – September 2016

ROMANCE

Morelli's Mistress	Anne Mather
A Tycoon to Be Reckoned With	Julia James
Billionaire Without a Past	Carol Marinelli
The Shock Cassano Baby	Andie Brock
The Most Scandalous Ravensdale	Melanie Milburne
The Sheikh's Last Mistress	Rachael Thomas
Claiming the Royal Innocent	Jennifer Hayward
The Billionaire Who Saw Her Beauty	Rebecca Winters
In the Boss's Castle	Jessica Gilmore
One Week with the French Tycoon	Christy McKellen
Rafael's Contract Bride	Nina Milne

HISTORICAL

In Bed with the Duke	Annie Burrows
More Than a Lover	Ann Lethbridge
Playing the Duke's Mistress	Eliza Redgold
The Blacksmith's Wife	Elisabeth Hobbes
That Despicable Rogue	Virginia Heath

MEDICAL

The Socialite's Secret	Carol Marinelli
London's Most Eligible Doctor	Annie O'Neil
Saving Maddie's Baby	Marion Lennox
A Sheikh to Capture Her Heart	Meredith Webber
Breaking All Their Rules	Sue MacKay
One Life-Changing Night	Louisa Heaton

0816 GEN STD LP

MILLS & BOON®

Why shop at millsandboon.co.uk?

Each year, thousands of romance readers find their
perfect read at millsandboon.co.uk. That's because
we're passionate about bringing you the very best
romantic fiction. Here are some of the advantages
of shopping at www.millsandboon.co.uk:

* **Get new books first**—you'll be able to buy your
  favourite books one month before they hit
  the shops

* **Get exclusive discounts**—you'll also be able to buy
  our specially created monthly collections, with up
  to 50% off the RRP

* **Find your favourite authors**—latest news,
  interviews and new releases for all your favourite
  authors and series on our website, plus ideas for
  what to try next

* **Join in**—once you've bought your favourite books,
  don't forget to register with us to rate, review and
  join in the discussions

Visit **www.millsandboon.co.uk**
for all this and more today!

MILLS_WEB_HB